REBELS OF THE RED PLANET

Originally published in 1961

By Charles Louis Fontenay

And the Special Bonus Story
AND NOW A MESSAGE . . .
By Greg Fowlkes

REBELS OF THE RED PLANET

© 2010 Resurrected Press
www.ResurrectedPress.com

Published by Resurrected Press

This classic book was handcrafted by Resurrected Press. Resurrected Press is dedicated to bringing high quality classic books back to the readers who enjoy them. These are not scanned versions of the originals, but, rather, quality checked and edited books meant to be enjoyed!

Please visit ResurrectedPress.com to view our entire catalogue!

ISBN 13: 978-1-935774-43-3

Printed in the United States of America

FOREWORD

Mars has always been a special place for science fiction writers. Before the first Mariner probes traveled the gulf between Earth and Mars, the Red Planet was a *tabla rossa* upon which authors could write anything they could imagine. Whether it was Edgar Rice Burroughs Barsoom of warriors and maidens, Robert Heinlein's more realistic *Red Planet*, or the sometimes whimsical Mars depicted in Ray Bradbury's *The Martian Chronicles*, Mars has served as a place where fantasies could be realized and political axes ground.

In *Rebels of the Red Planet* Charles Fontenay brings together a number of themes that were common in the science fiction of the fifties and early sixties. The first of these is a reaction to the conformity and consumer culture of the fifties. The monopolistic Marscorp serves to represent the faceless military industrial complex that seemed to dominate every facet of life in the fifties, from TV dinners to gigantic tailfins on cars.

The second is the idea that man was capable of a range of psychic abilities from telepathy to teleportation, if only his mind was freed from the constraints of his upbringing. For a time, there seemed to be some evidence for the truth of this idea. The experiments at the Rhine Institute for Parapsychology were receiving a lot of press, if not necessarily scientific credence. The belief that at least some individual could read minds, predict the future, or manipulate objects with their minds was widespread.

The third theme is that human evolution is not yet finished, that man is continuing to evolve both physically and mentally. The argument that the best way for man to survive in the hostile environments of alien planets was not to adapt them to his will, but to adapt himself to the environment, was a common theme in many science fiction stories and novels. The important question then became how would the adapted man interact with those who had not.

Fontenay has taken these three themes and woven them into a story set against a Mars that is not too far from what the best scientific guesses of the time indicated, a planet that was cold, dry, and with a an atmosphere too thin to breathe. The reality, of course, was that Mars was colder, dry, and with even less of an atmosphere than imagined. But it is the concepts, not the accuracy, of the author's imagination that is important.

Rebels of the Red Planet remains of interest, not because it paints a realistic picture of a future on Mars, but for the underlying story that it tells. Resurrected Press is pleased to offer it to our readers.

About the Author

Charles L. Fontenay (March 17, 1917 - January 27, 2007) was a newspaperman and science fiction writer. He served as editor of the Nashville Tennessean and worked for the Associated Press and Gannett News Service. In addition to science fiction, he wrote a biography of Estes Kefauver. His science fiction novels include *Twice Upon a Time, Rebels of the Red Planet*, and *The Day the Oceans Overflowed*.

Greg Fowlkes
Editor-In-Chief
Resurrected Press
www.ResurrectedPress.com

1

It is a sea, though they call it sand.

They call it sand because it is still and red and dense with grains. They call it sand because the thin wind whips it, and whirls its dusty skim away to the tight horizons of Mars.

But only a sea could so brood with the memory of aeons. Only a sea, lying so silent beneath the high skies, could hint the mystery of life still behind its barren veil.

To practical, rational man, it is the Xanthe Desert. Whatever else he might unwittingly be, S. Nuwell Eli considered himself a practical, rational man, and it was across the bumpy sands of the Xanthe Desert that he guided his groundcar westward with that somewhat cautious proficiency that mistrusts its own mastery of the machine. Maya Cara Nome, his colleague in this mission to which he had addressed himself, was a silent companion.

Nuwell's liquid brown eyes, insistent upon their visual clarity, saw the red sand as the blowing surface of unliving solidity. Only clarity was admitted to Nuwell, and the only living clarity was man and beast and vegetation, spotted in the dome cities and dome farms of the lowlands. He and Maya scurried, transiting sparks of the only life, insecure and hastening in the absence of the net of roads which eventually would bind the Martian surface to human reality from the toeholds of the dome cities.

In that opposite world which was the other side of the groundcar's seat, Maya Cara Nome's opaque black eyes struggled against the surface. They struggled not from any rational motivation but from long stubbornness, from habit, as a fly kicks six-legged and constant against the surface tension of a trapping pool.

Formally, Maya was allied to Newell's clarity and solidity, and she could express this alliance with complete logic if called on. But behind the casually blowing sand she sensed a depth. The shimmering atmosphere, hostile to man, which sealed the red desert was a lens that distorted and concealed by its intervention. The groundcar was a mechanical bug, an alienness with which timorous man had allied himself; allied with it against reality, she and Nuwell were hastened by it through reality, unseeing, toward the goal of a more comfortable unreality.

The groundcar bumped and slithered, and an orange dust-cloud boiled up from its broad tires and wafted away across the sculpted sand. The desert stretched away, silent and empty, to the distant horizon; the groundcar the only humming disturbance of its silence and emptiness. The steel-blue sky shimmered above, a lens capping the red surface.

The groundcar rolled westward, slashing toward its goal from the distant lowland of Solis Lacus. Far away, two men, machineless, plodded this same Xanthe Desert toward the same goal; but they plodded southward, approaching on a different radius.

They were naked. In a thin atmosphere without sufficient oxygen to support animal life or even the higher forms of terrestrial plant life, they wore no marsuits, no helmets, no oxygen tanks.

The man who walked in front was tall, erect, powerfully muscled. His features and short-clipped hair were coarse, but self-assured intelligence shone in his smoky eyes. He moved across the loose sand, barefoot, with easy grace.

The–man?–that shambled behind him was as tall, but appeared shorter and even more muscular because his shoulders and head were hunched forward. His even coarser face was characterized by vacuously slack mouth and blue eyes empty of any expression except an occasional brief frown of puzzlement.

Toward a focal point: from the east, two people; from the north, two people. If in the efficient self-assurance of Adam Hennessey could be paralleled a variant harmony with the insistent surfaceness of S. Nuwell Eli, does any coincidental parallelism exist between Brute Hennessey and Maya Cara Nome?

Puzzlement was the climate of Brute's mind. This surface film of things through which he ploughed his way, the swarming currents below the surface–all were chaos. He grasped vaguely at comprehension without achieving, the effective coalescence of electric ideas always falling short before reaching consciousness.

The two men plodded, naked, through the loose sand. Above them in the Mars-blue dome of day, the weak sun turned downward, warning of its eventual departure.

A two-passengered groundcar and two men, widely apart, and yet bound for the same destination....

The destination was a lone, sprawling building in the desert. It could have been a huge warehouse, or a fortress, of black, almost windowless Martian stone. The only outstanding feature of its virtually featureless hulk was a tower which struck upward from its northern side.

As the summer afternoon progressed, Dr. G. O. T. Hennessey paced the windy summit of the tower, peered frequently into the desert north beneath a sunshading hand, and waggled his goat beard in annoyance under his transparent marshelmet.

Had the helmet speaker been on or the air less thin, one might have determined that Goat Hennessey was utilizing some choice profanity, directed at those two absent personages whose names were, respectively, Adam and Brute.

The airlock to the tower elevator opened and a small creature–a child?–emerged onto the roof. Distorted, humpbacked and barrel-chested, it scuttled on reed-thin legs to Goat's side. It wore no marsuit.

"Father!" screeched this apparition, its thin voice curiously muffled by the tenuous air. "Petway fell in the laundry vat!"

"For the love of space!" muttered Goat in exasperation. "Is there water in it?"

When the newcomer gave no sign of hearing, Goat realized his helmet speaker was off. He switched it on.

"Is there water in the vat?" he repeated.

"Yes, sir. It's full of suds and clothes."

"Well, go fish him out before he soaks up all the water. The soap will make him sick."

The messenger turned, almost tripping over its own broad feet, and went back through the airlock. Goat returned to his northward vigil.

Miles away, Nuwell slowed the groundcar as it approached the lip of that precipitous slope bordering the short canal which connects Juventae Fons with the Arorae Sinus Lowland. He consulted a rough chart, and turned the groundcar southward. A drive of about a kilometer brought them to a wide descending ledge down which they were able to drive into the canal.

Here, on the flat lowland surface, the canal sage grew thick, a gray-green expanse stretching unbroken to the distant cliff that was the other side of the canal. Occasionally above its smoothness thrust the giant barrel of a canal cactus.

Nuwell headed the groundcar straight across the canal, for the chart showed that the nearest upward ledge on the other side was conveniently almost opposite. The big wheels bent and crushed the canal sage, leaving a double trail.

The canal sage brought with it the comforting feeling of surface life once more. This feeling, for no reason that he could have determined consciously, released Nuwell's tongue.

"Maya," he said, in a voice that betrayed determination behind its mildness, "I don't see any real reason for waiting. When we've cleared up this matter at Ultra Vires and get back to Mars City, I think we should get married."

She glanced at his handsome profile and smiled affectionately.

"I'm complimented by your impatience, Nuwell," she said. "But there is a good reason for waiting, for me. When we're married, I want to be your wife, completely. I want to keep your home and mother your children. Don't you understand that?"

"That's what I want, too," he said. "That's my idea of what marriage is. But, Maya, if you insist on finishing this government assignment, that could be a long time off."

"I know, and I don't like it any better than you do, darling," said Maya. "But it's cost the Earth government a great deal of trouble and money to send me here, and you know how long it would take for them to get a replacement to Mars for me. I don't feel that I can let them down, and I don't think it would be much of a beginning to our marriage for me to be running around ferreting out rebels during the first months of it."

"That's another thing I don't like, Maya," said Nuwell. "It's dangerous, and I don't want anything to happen to you."

"It's your work, too, and it's not absolutely safe for you, either. I'll be sharing it with you when we're married, and for you it will go on for a long time. I have a specific mission here, to locate the rebel headquarters, and as soon as I've done that I'll be more than happy to become just a contented housewife and leave the rest of it to you."

Nuwell shrugged, a little disconsolately, and turned his attention to the task of negotiating the groundcar up the ascending slope.

She was a strange creature, this little Maya of his. She had been born on Mars and, orphaned by some unknown disaster, had been cared for during her first years by the mysterious, grotesque native Martians. When they took her at last to one of the dome cities, she was sent to Earth for rearing. And now she was back on Mars as an undercover agent of the Earth government, seeking to ferret out the rebels known to be engaging in widespread forbidden activities.

Often he did not understand her, but he wanted her, nevertheless.

Nuwell steered the groundcar slowly up the slope, over rubble and ruts, avoiding the largest rocks. At last they reached the top, and the groundcar arrowed out over the desert again, picking up speed.

Far to the left and ahead of them there was another dust-cloud drifting up, one that was not of the thin wind, but nearly stationary. Nuwell found the binoculars in the storage compartment and handed them to Maya.

"What's that over there?" he wondered. "Another groundcar? Take a look, Maya."

Maya trained the glasses in the direction indicated, through the groundcar's transparent dome. It was difficult to get them focused, for the groundcar swayed and jolted, but at last she was able to make brief identification.

"They're Martians, Nuwell," she said. "Can we drive over that way?"

"You've seen Martians before," he said.

"But I'd like to speak with them," she said. "I talk their language, you know."

"Yes, I do know, darling, but that's utterly foolish. They're only animals, after all, and we have to get to Ultra Vires before night, if we can."

He kept the groundcar on its course.

Maya lapsed into disgruntled silence. Nuwell stole a sidelong glance at her, his breath catching slightly at the curve of the petite, perfectly feminine form beneath the loose Martian tunic and baggy trousers. He reached over and patted her hand.

But Maya was offended. She kept her black head turned away from him, looking out of the groundcar dome across the desert.

At their destination, Goat Hennessey peered eagerly into the distance, searching.

This time, his watery blue eyes picked up two tiny figures on the horizon. He watched them as they approached, finally detailing themselves into two naked, pink creatures of manshape and only slightly more than mansize.

"They made it," he muttered. "Both of them. Good!"

He turned and entered the airlock. As soon as its air reached terrestrial density and composition, he removed his marshelmet.

Goat rode the elevator to the ground level, left it and hurried down a corridor, reaching the outside airlock in time to admit the two figures.

Adam entered first, easily confident, carrying his head like a king. Brute shambled behind him.

"Everything go all right?" asked Goat, his voice quavering in his anxiety.

"Fine, father," said Adam, smiling to reveal savage, even teeth.

"Nothing unusual happen?"

"Nothing at all, sir."

"You forget, Adam?" mouthed Brute eagerly. "You forget you fall?"

Adam spun on him ferociously, raising a heavy hand in threat. Brute did not cringe.

"I forget nothing!" snarled Adam. "You crazy Brute, I say it is nothing!"

"But, Adam—"

"I say it is nothing!" howled Adam and sprang for him.

"Stop it!" snapped Goat, like the crack of a whip, and they froze in the moment of their grappling. Sheepishly, they parted and stood side by side before him.

"I'll listen to details after supper," said Goat. "The children are hungry, and so am I."

2

Adam and Brute followed Goat Hennessey down the corridor, towering over him like Saint Bernards on the heels of a terrier. They turned into the dining room, a big square room centered with a rude table and chairs, one wall pierced by a fireplace in which a big cauldron steamed over smouldering coals.

The dining room swarmed with a dozen small creatures, human in their pink flesh, more or less human in their twisted bodies. As soon as Goat entered with Adam and Brute in tow, the assemblage set up a high-pitched howling and twittering of anticipation and began beating utensils on the dishes, table and walls.

"Quiet!" squawked Goat over the tremendous clatter, and the noise subsided. They stood where they were, bright eyes fixed on him.

These were "the children." Some of them were humpbacked, like Evan, the one who had carried the message to the tower. Some, like Evan, were grotesquely barrel-chested, with or without the hump. Some were as thin as skeletons, with huge heads; some were hulking miniatures of Brute. One steatopygean girl was so bulky in legs and hindquarters that she could waddle only a few inches with each step, yet her head and upper torso were skinny and fragile.

Goat sat down at the head of the table, and immediately there was a tumbling rush for places. Most of the children sat, chattering, while two of the larger girls moved around the table, taking bowls to the cauldron, filling them with a brownish stew and returning them.

They ate in silence. When supper was ended, the children scattered, some to play, others to chores. Goat beckoned to Adam and Brute to follow him. He led them down the corridor and into his study.

Goat turned on the light, revealing a book-lined, paper-stacked room focused on a huge desk. He removed his marsuit to stand in baggy trousers and loose tunic. Adam and Brute stood near the door, shifting uncomfortably, for the study was normally forbidden ground.

Goat stood by a thick double window, looking out over the desert to the west. The small sun disappeared beneath the horizon even as he looked, leaving the fast-darkening sky a dull, faint red. Almost as though released by the sunset, pale Phobos popped above the horizon and began to climb its eastward way. The desert already was dark, but a stirring above it bespoke a distant sandstorm.

Goat turned from the window and faced the pair.

"Well," he snapped harshly, "what happened?"

Adam smiled confidently.

"We did as you said, father," he answered. "We walked to the edge of the canal, and we walked back. We had no water and we had no air. We did not feel tired. We did not feel sick."

"Fine! Fine!" murmured Goat.

"Father ..." said Brute.

Goat turned his eyes to Brute, and savage irritation swept over him. With that word, at that moment, Brute gave him a feeling of guilty foreboding.

"Don't call me 'father!'" snapped Goat angrily.

"But you say call you father," protested Brute, the puzzled frown wrinkling his brow. "What I call you if I not call you father?"

"Don't call me anything. Say 'sir.' What did you want to say?"

"Father, sir," began Brute again, "Adam forget. Adam fall."

With a muted roar, Adam swept his powerful arm in a backhanded arc that caught Brute full on the side of his head. The blow would have felled an ox, but Brute was not shaken. Apparently unhurt, he stood patiently, his blue eyes on Goat with something of pleading in them.

"Adam, let him alone!" commanded Goat sharply.

"Brute, what do you mean, Adam fell?"

"We come back. We not far from canal. Adam fall. Adam sick. Adam turn blue."

"It is lies, father!" exclaimed Adam, glaring at Brute. "It is not true."

"Let him finish," instructed Goat. "I'll decide whether it's true. What did you do, Brute?"

"I find cactus, father," answered Brute. "I make hole in cactus. I put Adam inside. I put hole back. Adam stay in cactus. Then Adam break cactus and come out again. We come back."

Goat cogitated. If Adam had shown, symptoms of oxygen starvation.... The big canal cacti were hollow, and in their interiors they maintained reserves of oxygen for their own use. More than once, such a cactus had saved a Martian traveler's life when his oxygen supply ran short.

He turned to Adam.

"Well, Adam?" he asked.

"I tell you, father, it is lies! I do not fall. Brute does not put me in the cactus."

"And why should he lie?" asked Goat blandly.

This stumped Adam for a minute. Then he brightened.

"Brute wants to be bigger and stronger than Adam," he said. "Brute knows Adam is bigger and stronger than Brute, Brute does not like this. He tells you lies so you will think Brute is bigger and stronger than Adam."

"I know you are bigger brother, Adam," objected Brute, almost plaintively. "I not try to be bigger. Why you say you do not fall?"

"I do not fall!" howled Adam. "I do not fall, you stupid Brute!"

Goat held up a stern hand, enforcing silence.

"I can't certainly settle this disagreement, but I'd be inclined to accept what Brute says," said Goat thoughtfully. "You're smart enough to lie, Adam. Brute isn't. The only thing I can do is to run the experiment over. You shall go out again tomorrow, and this time I'll go with you."

"You'll see, father," said Adam confidently. "Adam will not fall."

"Perhaps not. But I must be sure. As much as I prefer your more human characteristics, Adam, it's entirely possible that Brute has some survival qualities that you lack."

"Is true, father," said Brute eagerly. "Some things kill Adam, they not kill Brute."

"You lie!" cried Adam again, turning on him. "Why do you lie, Brute?"

"No lie," insisted Brute. "You know, is true."

"Lie! Lie!" shouted Adam. "Adam is bigger and stronger! What do you say can kill Adam that does not kill Brute?"

"This," replied Brute calmly.

With an unhurried lunge, he picked up a heavy knife from Goat's desk. In a single easy movement, he turned and slashed Adam's throat neatly.

Choking and gurgling, Adam sank to his knees, bright blood spouting from his neck, while Goat stood frozen in horror. Adam fell prone, he kicked and threshed convulsively like a beheaded chicken, then twitched and lay still in a spreading pool of blood.

Brute calmly wiped the knife on his naked thigh and laid it back on the desk.

"Adam dead," he said without emotion. "Brute not lie."

Dismayed fury erupted through Goat's veins and a red haze swept over his eyes.

"You idiot!" he squawked. "So that won't kill you?"

Goaded beyond endurance, Goat seized the knife and swung it as hard as he could against Brute's neck. It thunked like an ax biting into a tree trunk, biting halfway through the flesh. Brute recoiled at the impact, tearing the handle from Goat's feeble hands and leaving the knife blade stuck in his throat.

Brute staggered momentarily. Then he reached up and jerked the knife away. Blood spurted through his severed throat. Brute clapped a hand to the wound, tightly.

For a moment, blood oozed through his fingers. Then, pale but steady, Brute dropped his hand.

The wound had closed! Its edges already were sealed, leaving a raw, red scar that no longer bled.

"Brute not lie," said Brute, the words forced out with some difficulty. "It not kill Brute."

Stunned by astonishment and disbelief, Goat stared at him, his mouth moving soundlessly.

"Go away," he whispered hoarsely at last. "Go out of here, monster!"

Obediently, Brute shambled out of the study. As he passed through the door, Goat regained his voice and called after him:

"Tell the children to come and take away Adam's body."

*   *   *   *   *

Kilometers away, Maya Cara Nome and S. Nuwell Eli rode a groundcar that moved swiftly across the interminable waves of the red sand. It swayed through hollows and jounced over multiple ridges, Nuwell steering it with some difficulty. In the steely sky, the small sun moved downward, its brightness unimpaired by the occasional thin clouds which moved before it.

The sun touched the western horizon, seemed to hesitate, dropped with breathtaking suddenness, and the stars immediately began to appear in the deepening twilight sky.

They stopped and had a compact meal, heated in the groundcar's short-wave cooker. Then Nuwell switched on the headlights and they went on again.

Soon afterward, a faint spot of light appeared in the desert far ahead of them. As they approached it, it became a yellow-lighted window in a huge black mass rearing up against the night sky. They had reached Ultra Vires.

Nuwell announced their arrival over the groundcar radio and swung the groundcar up beside the building's main entrance. He sealed the groundcar's door to the building air-lock so they would not have to don marsuits.

After a few moments, the airlock opened. They passed through it and were greeted by a skinny, shriveled little man with watery blue eyes and a goatee.

"I was expecting you, but not tonight," said this person, rather sourly. "Well, come on in and I'll have the children fix you something to eat if you haven't eaten."

"I'm S. Nuwell Eli," said Nuwell, holding out a hand which the other ignored. "This is the terrestrial agent, Miss Maya Cara Nome. You are Dr. Hennessey, I assume."

"That's right," said Goat. "Do you want supper?"

"No, thank you, we ate on the way," said Nuwell. "I'd like to get started with the inspection as soon as possible."

"Inspection or investigation?" suggested Goat, sniffling. "Well, no matter. I have nothing to hide."

He led them down a dim, dusty corridor, stretching deep into the dark bowels of the building, and turned aside into a paper-stacked room which evidently was his study. He went straight to a big desk, sat down, swivelled his chair around and waved them to seats. Nuwell shuffled a little uncomfortably, then sank into a chair, but Maya remained standing by the door, her small traveling bag in her hand, indignation rising in her.

"Before you settle down to charts and questions, Dr. Hennessey, do you mind showing us to our rooms so we may wash away some of the travel dust?" she asked icily, black eyes snapping.

At this, Goat jumped to his feet, sincere contrition in his face wiping out all traces of his irritated gruffness.

"I'm very sorry!" he exclaimed. "I hope you will forgive my manners, but I've lived and worked here alone in the desert so long that I had forgotten the niceties of civilization."

This apology cleared the air. Goat showed them their overnight quarters, adjoining rooms which were not luxurious but were reasonably comfortable, and after a time the three of them congregated once more in Goat's study, all of them in better humor.

"Let us have some wine first," suggested Goat. "This is very good red wine, imported from Earth."

He went to the door and shouted into the corridor.

"Petway!"

Goat returned to his chair. A few moments later, a twittering noise sounded in the corridor, then a horrible little apparition appeared in the door. It was a child-sized creature, naked, grotesquely barrel-chested and teetering on thin, twisted legs. Its hairless head was skull-like, with gaping mouth and huge, round eyes.

Maya gasped, profoundly shocked. The little creature looked more like a miniature Martian native than a human, but the Martians themselves were not so distorted. She saw her own shock reflected in Nuwell's face.

"Petway, get us three glasses of wine," commanded Goat calmly.

Petway vanished and Goat turned briskly back to his guests.

"Now," he said, "I shall outline the progress of my experiments to you and answer any questions you may have."

3

Maya's education was extensive, but it did not include the genetic sciences. She was able to follow Goat's explanations and his references to the charts he hung, one after another, on the wall of his study, but she was able to follow them only in a general sense. The technical details escaped her.

Nuwell seemed to have a better grasp of the subject. He nodded his dark, curly head frequently, and occasionally asked a question or two.

"Surgery is performed with a concentrated electron stream on the cells of the early embryo," said Goat. "I call it surgery, but actually it is an alteration of the structure of certain specific genes which govern the characteristics I am attempting to change. Such changes would, of course, then be transmitted on down to any progeny.

"The earlier the embryo is caught, the easier and surer the surgery, because when it has divided into too many cells the very task of dealing with each one separately makes the time requirement prohibitive, besides multiplying the chance for error. The Martians have a method of altering the physical structure and genetic composition of a full-grown adult, but this is far beyond the stage I've reached."

"The Martians?" repeated Nuwell in astonishment. "You mean the Martian natives? They're nothing but degenerated animals!"

"You're wrong," replied Goat. "I know that's the general opinion, but I had considerable contact with them a good many years ago. Perhaps most of them are little more than strange animals. No one really knows. They live simple, animal-like lives, holed up in desert caves, and they're rarely communicative in any way. But I know from my own experience that some of them, at least, are still familiar with that ancient science that they must have possessed when Earth was in an earlier stage of life than the human."

"This ... child ... that brought us the wine is one of the products of your experiments?" asked Nuwell.

"Yes. Petway's pretty representative of the children, I'm afraid. I've been trying to determine what went wrong. It could be an inaccuracy in dealing with the genetic structure itself, or a failure to follow exactly the same pattern of change in moving from one cell to another in the embryo. If I could only catch one at the single cell stage!

"None of the children has turned out as well as my first two experiments, Brute and Adam. Both of them were born about twenty-five years ago–terrestrial years, that is–and developed into normal, even superior physical specimens. Unfortunately, their mental development was retarded. Adam was the brighter of the two, and Brute killed him tonight, shortly before your arrival."

Maya shivered.

"Somehow, it seems horrible to me, experimenting with human lives this way," she said.

"It's being done for a good cause, Maya," said Nuwell. "Dr. Hennessey's objective is to help man live better on Mars. After all, there is nothing nobler than the individual's sacrifice of himself for his fellows, whether it's voluntary or involuntary."

"But what about the mothers of these children?" asked Maya.

"The big problem is to reach them as soon as possible after conception," said Goat, misinterpreting her question. "We do this by magnetic detectors, which report instantly the conjunction of the positive and negative. The surgery is performed, as quickly as possible, utilizing the suspended animation technique which is being developed toward interstellar travel."

"I wasn't asking about the technical aspects," said Maya. "What I want to know is, what sort of mothers will permit you to experiment this way on their unborn children, especially seeing the results you've already obtained?"

Goat started to answer, but Nuwell forestalled him.

"There are some things that are none of your business, darling," he said. "The terrestrial government sent you here on a specific assignment, and I don't think you should inquire into matters which are classified as secret by the local government, which don't have anything to do with that assignment. Now, Dr. Hennessey, just what sort of survival qualities have you been able to develop in these experiments?"

"There's no witchcraft involved," retorted Goat, with a sardonic grimace.

"I haven't accused you," said Nuwell quickly.

"No, but I keep up with events, even out here, well enough to know that you're the Mars City government's chief nemesis where there's any suspicion of extrasensory perception. I doubt that you chose to make this trip yourself without reason, Mr. Eli."

"It's merely a routine inspection," murmured Nuwell.

Goat indicated one of his charts, showing a diagram of genes and chromosomes in different colors.

"This is my original chart," he said. "I copied it from one belonging to the Martians many years ago, and my genetic alteration of Brute and Adam were based on it. But I must have miscopied it, or else the Martians didn't have the objective I thought they did in it, because I could find no alteration of genes affecting lung capacity or oxygen utilization. My own subsequent charts, on which later experiments were based, are alterations of this."

"But just what is your objective, and how well have you succeeded?" persisted Nuwell.

"Ability to survive under Martian conditions."

"I know. This is stated in all previous inspection reports. I want something more specific."

"Why, ability to survive in an almost oxygen-free atmosphere, of course. As well as can be determined, the Martians do this by deriving oxygen from surface solids and storing it in their humps under compression, very much like an oxygen tank.

"I've succeeded to some degree with my children. All of them can go an hour or two without breathing. What I don't understand is that no capacities like that were included in the genetic changes on Adam and Brute, and yet they've gradually developed an ability to do much better. Both of them were out on the desert the entire day today without oxygen."

Nuwell was silent for a moment, tapping the tips of his fingers together, apparently in deep thought. Then he said:

"Maya, I think we've reached the point where you had better retire to your room and let us to talk privately. You can question Dr. Hennessey in the morning about any attempts the rebels may have made to contact him."

Maya obeyed silently, rather glad to get away and think things over alone. When she had come to Mars as an agent of the Earth government, it had not occurred to her that there would be areas of information from which the local government would bar her. She recognized that such a prohibition was perfectly valid, but she was a little offended, nevertheless.

Her room was a spacious one on the ground level, and boasted one of Ultra Vires' few large windows. Maya unpacked her bag, and gratefully stripped off her boots and socks, her tunic and baggy trousers. In underpants, she went into the small bathroom, washed cosmetics from her face and brushed down her thick, short hair.

Donning her light sleeping garment, she sat down on the edge of her bed. She was very tired from the long drive and, almost without thinking, she did not get up to turn out the light. She thought at it.

The switch clicked and the light went out.
She felt foolish and a little frightened. She had never
told Nuwell of this sort of thing. Can a woman ask her
witch-hunting lover: "Do you think I'm a witch?"
With almost total recall, as though she heard it
spoken, she remembered the summation speech Nuwell
had made the first time she had seen him in action. He
was prosecuting a man charged with conducting
experiments similar to the historic and outlawed Rhine
experiments of Earth.

*"Gentlemen, we sit here in a public building and
conduct certain necessary human affairs in a dignified
and orderly manner. We follow a way of life we brought
with us from distant Earth. Apparently, we are as safe
here as we would be on Earth.*

*"I say 'apparently.' Sometimes we forget the thin
barriers here that protect us against disaster, against
extermination. A rent in this city's dome, a failure in our
oxygen machinery, a clogging of our pumping system by
the ever-present sand, and most of us would die before
help could reach us from our nearest neighbors.*

*"We live here under certain restrictions that many of
us do not like. Certainly, no one likes to be unable to step
out under the open sky without wearing a bulky marsuit
and an oxygen tank. Certainly, no one likes to be rationed
on water and meat throughout the foreseeable future.*

*"But what we have to remember is that absolute
discipline has always been a requirement for those
courageous souls in the vanguard of human progress.*

*"Witchcraft–the practice of extrasensory perception, if
you prefer the term–is forbidden on Mars because to
practice it one must differ from his fellow men when the
inexorable dangers of our frontier demand that we work
together. To practice it, one must devote time and mental
effort to untried things when our thin margin of safety
makes concentrated and combined effort necessary for
survival. That is why witchcraft is forbidden on Mars.*

"Let those who yet cling to the wistful liberalism of Earth label us conformists if they will. I say to you that until Mars is won for humanity, we cannot afford the luxury of nonconformity.

"Gentlemen, I give you the prosecution's case."

Maya stared out the window. This whole side of Ultra Vires was dark, except for a rectangle of light cast from a window a little distance away—the window of Goat Hennessey's study. In this rectangle, the red sand of the desert lay clear and stark.

Near the end of the rectangle lay an indistinct, crumpled, oblong figure. Puzzled, Maya studied it. It looked like a body to her.

*   *   *   *   *

In the study, Nuwell gazed at the skinny doctor with angry brown eyes.

"The bulletins sent to you, as well as other researchers, gave specific instructions that research was to be directed toward human utilization of certain foods now being developed," accused Nuwell.

"I thought this was more important," replied Goat.

"You thought! You're not on Earth, where scientists can get government grants and go jaunting off on wild research projects of their own."

"I still think this is more important," said Goat stubbornly. "I know that all of us are expected to co-operate and stick to tried and accepted lines so we won't be wasting time and material. Perhaps I was wrong in not doing that initially. But now I've proved that this line of research can be followed profitably, so its continuance now can't be looked on as a waste of time."

"Scientists should leave political direction to more experienced men," said Nuwell in an exasperated tone. "This is not merely a matter of time waste, or nonconformity. The Mars Corporation operates our sole supply line to Earth, Dr. Hennessey, and that supply line brings to man on Mars all the many things he needs to live here. The Earth-Mars run is an expensive operation, and it's important that it remain economically feasible for Marscorp to operate it.

"No matter how altruistic you may be about it, you get man to the point that he doesn't depend on atmospheric oxygen here, and domes, pressurized houses and groundcars, oxygen equipment–a great many things are going to be unnecessary. But there'll still be a lot of other things we'll have to have from Earth. Don't you realize what a disaster it would be if Marscorp decided to drop the only spaceship line to Earth because its cargo fell off to the point that it was economically unsound?"

Goat looked at him with shrewd blue eyes.

"I think I can jump to a conclusion," he remarked mildly. "Marscorp has some sort of control over the 'foods' you're trying to make practical for human consumption in the approved experiments, doesn't it?"

"Well, yes. Marscorp wants to make man gradually self-sufficient on Mars, and I think it's legitimate that Marscorp derive some economic benefits from its efforts in that direction."

"I've wondered for some time just how close Marscorp and the government were tied together," said Goat dryly. "Obviously, if I don't do as you say, my supplies here will be cut off. So I have no choice but to discontinue this work and turn my attention to the approved line."

"That isn't quite adequate now," said Nuwell. "You're going to have to leave here and come to Mars City where you can do your research under supervision. Your experimental humans here will be destroyed, of course."

"Destroyed?" There was an agonized note to Goat's voice. "All of them? How about the two mothers I have who haven't given birth yet?"

"You'd destroy them anyhow, as you have the others, not long after the births. And that brings up another thing. When you get to Mars City, watch your tongue. You almost revealed to Miss Cara Nome that the government has been kidnapping an expectant mother now and then for your experiments."

"Years of work, gone to waste," mourned Goat somberly. "When must I do this?"

"As soon as possible. You'll be expected in Mars City within two weeks. Now, I'd like to see these experimental humans."

A few moments later, they made their way together through a large dormitory in which all of Goat's charges were sleeping. Nuwell shuddered at the sight of the small, deformed bodies.

"I don't worry that you could ever take any of these to Mars City undetected. But," he said, pointing to Brute, "that one looks too near normal. I want to see him destroyed before I leave."

"Brute? But he's the most successful one I have left!"

"Exactly. That's why I want to see him destroyed, tonight."

Goat awoke Brute, and the monster man sleepily followed them back to the study.

Goat picked up the huge knife, still stained with Adam's blood, and looked Brute squarely in the face. Brute returned the gaze, no comprehension in his dull blue eyes.

"You think I can't kill you, Brute?" said Goat coldly. "I'll show you!"

With a surgeon's precision, Goat plunged the sharp point between Brute's ribs and into the heart.

Shock swept over Brute's mind.

Father kills me!

Reject! Reject!

Father, all kindness, all hope, all wisdom and love, wants me no more. Father rejects me! Father kills me!

Despair!

Reject! Reject!
Blackness swept fading through Brute's despairing
brain.
One agonized note of pleading in the pale-blue eyes,
and they closed in acceptance. Brute swayed and fell
forward, crashing to the floor, driving the knife into his
chest to the hilt.
Brute shuddered and rolled over on his back. He lay
sprawled, arms flung out limply, the knife hilt protruding
upward. He sighed, and his breathing stopped.
Goat stared down at him. He picked up Brute's wrist
and held it. There was no pulse.

* * * * *

Shortly after dawn, Maya awoke. Remembering what
she had seen dimly the night before, she went curiously
to the window.
There were two of them now. They were bodies,
human bodies, naked and unquestionably dead. In the
night, the dry, vampirish Martian air had dessicated
them. They were skeletons, parchment skin stretched
tightly over the lifeless bones.
Even as she stood and looked, a group of figures
appeared on the horizon and came slowly nearer. They
were Martians—monstrous creatures, huge-chested,
humpbacked, with tremendously long, thin legs and
arms, their big-eyed, big-eared heads mere excrescences
in front of their humps.
Trailing slowly through the desert toward Aurorae
Sinus, they passed near the skeleton bodies. One of the
Martians saw them. He boomed excitedly at the others,
loudly enough for Maya to hear through the double
window.

The Martians stopped and gathered around the bodies.

What, she wondered, could interest them in two corpses? There was no guessing. Martian motives and thought processes were alien and incomprehensible, even to one who had lived among them and communicated with them as a child.

One of the Martians picked up one of the corpses, and the whole group moved away toward the lowland, the Martian carrying the body easily with one long-fingered hand. Wisps of sandy dust trailed them as they dwindled and slowly vanished.

The second body lay where they had left it. A gaping wound in its throat seemed to mock her.

4

Fancher Laddigan made his way down a long dim corridor in the rear portion of the Childress Barber College, in Mars City's eastern quarter. He stopped and hesitated, with some trepidation, before an unmarked door near the end of the corridor.

Completely bald, bespectacled and well up in years, Fancher looked like a clerk and he had the instincts of a clerk. Yet he utilized that appearance and those instincts in a perilous cause.

Fancher knocked timidly on the door. On receiving an indistinct invitation from inside, he pushed it open and entered.

Fancher had a tendency to shiver every time he had occasion to see the Chief, whose real name was unknown to Fancher and to most others here at the barber college.

Small as a child in body, wagging a thin-haired head larger than lifesize, the Chief surveyed Fancher with icy green eyes. The eyes were large and round as a child's, but there was nothing childlike about their expression. As though to deny his physical smallness, he smoked one of the fragrant, foot-long cigars produced only in the Hadriacum Lowlands.

"Sit down," commanded the Chief in a high, piping voice.

Fancher swallowed and sat, facing his superior across the big desk. The Chief opened a drawer, took out another of the long cigars, and handed it to Fancher. Fancher did not like cigars, but he had never dared say so to the Chief. He lit it gingerly, coughed at his first inhalation, and smoked at it dutifully and unhappily.

"You recognized this man certainly as Dark Kensington?" asked the Chief.

"Well ..." Fancher began, and started coughing again. The Chief fixed him with an unwinking green stare. When the coughing spell ended, Fancher sat silent, his eyes stinging with tears, fumbling at what he wanted to say.

"You knew Dark Kensington before his disappearance twenty-five years ago," said the Chief, with a trace of impatience in his tone. "I am told that you saw this man and talked to him. You are qualified to recognize Dark Kensington. Is this man Dark Kensington, or not?"

"Well," said Fancher again, "the man was walking alone across the desert, and when someone picked him up he asked how he could find the Childress Barber College, and of course our men heard of it and went out to—"

"I have received a full report on the man's appearance and our initial contact with him. I asked you a question."

"Well, Chief, it's a peculiar thing. If this man, as he is now, had reappeared twenty-five years ago, I'd *know* it was Dark Kensington. But he looks exactly as Dark did when he disappeared, not one day older. And he doesn't remember a thing beyond his disappearance except events of the past two weeks, he says.

"Yet his memories of Dark's activities before his disappearance are unquestionably accurate and clear. It's as though Dark had been put on ice at the time of his disappearance and just now thawed out, without any aging or memory during the interim."

"Perhaps he was," said the Chief dryly. "But is it possible that this man, looking so much like Dark Kensington, could have studied Kensington's personality and activities carefully and be posing as Kensington?"

"No, sir," said Fancher promptly. "Dark and I were very close friends at one time. He remembers that, although he had difficulty recognizing me since I'm so much older. We went through some experiences together that I never told to anyone, and I'm sure he didn't. He remembers them in every detail. Like the way we trapped a sage-rabbit once when we'd run out of supplies out in Hadriacum."

Fancher chuckled.

"Then we couldn't eat the thing," he reminisced.

"Very well, if you're sure of his identity, that's all I wish to know," said the Chief. "I don't want to be trapped by a Marscorp trick with plastic surgery. But if this man is Dark Kensington, it's the best fortune the Phoenix has met with in a long time."

He fell silent, and busied himself with papers on his desk, paying no more attention to Fancher. Fancher waited, then concluded reasonably that the interview was at an end. And, since the long cigar agonized him, he rose and moved quietly toward the door.

"I have not given you permission to leave," said the Chief, without raising either his eyes or his voice. "Kensington is due to arrive in a few moments, and I want you here when I talk to him. If any of his words or actions appear inconsistent in any way to you, I want you to let me know."

Fancher sighed silently, returned to his chair and puffed disconsolately on the cigar.

Some five minutes passed. Then there was a firm rap on the door.

"Come in!" called the Chief in his reedy voice.

The door opened, and in walked a man whose entire presence radiated strength, confidence and the potentiality of instant violence. Dark Kensington was tall and broad-shouldered, clad in dark-blue tunic and baggy trousers. His face was darkly tanned, strong, handsome. His hair was black as midnight. His eyes were startlingly pale in the dark face; eyes of pale blue, remote and filled with light.

"I'm Dark Kensington," he said, striding up to the Chief's desk. "You're the man known as the Chief?"

"Yes," answered the Chief, and waited.

Dark nodded to Fancher. Fancher, feeling rather green about the gills, returned the greeting.

Dark turned his attention back to the Chief, and he, also, waited. There was a long silence. The Chief broke it first.

"What do you know about Dr. G. O. T. Hennessey— Goat Hennessey?" asked the Chief calmly.

Fancher blinked at this unexpected line of questioning. A cloud passed over Dark's face, as though the name had triggered something in him that he could not quite remember.

"He was a very good friend of mine," answered Dark, "although it seems that something happened between us that I can't quite recollect. He was one of the most brilliant geneticists of Earth, and came to Mars with an experimental group that was to try to develop a human type that could live more comfortably under Martian conditions. The project was backed by the government."

He stopped. It was the Chief who added:

"Then Marscorp stepped in."

The expression on Dark's face was blank.

"You don't know what Marscorp is, do you?" asked the Chief curiously.

"The name's familiar," replied Dark. "It's a spaceline, isn't it?"

"If your amnesia is genuine, you might very well react in such a fashion," said the Chief reflectively. "Marscorp is the Mars Corporation, and it's the only spaceline that serves Mars now. It's a giant combine on Earth which has a virtual monopoly on the spacelines and exports and imports between Earth and all the colonized planets.

"Marscorp is against any development of human beings who can live under natural extraterrestrial conditions, because that would end the colonies' dependence on Marscorp for supplies. As it is, the colonies literally can't live without Marscorp. Marscorp controls enough senators and delegates in the World Congress to block other important projects if the Earth government refuses to co-operate with it, so the government–that is to say, Marscorp–put a ban on the experiments by Hennessey and other scientists here."

"I remember the government ban on the projects, but I wasn't aware that Marscorp had anything to do with it," said Dark. "Goat Hennessey was one of a group of us who retired to the desert to continue work despite the government ban."

"Goat sold out," said the Chief. "Perhaps your memory doesn't include that important point, but Fancher remembers it well. It was a little before my time. Goat sold out, and betrayed the others to the government in return for assistance in carrying out more limited experiments. Some of the group escaped and formed the nucleus of the rebel movement which now is centered here at the Childress Barber College. We call ourselves the Order of the Phoenix."

The Chief allowed himself the luxury of a very faint smile.

"Marscorp and the government call us the Desert Rats," he said. "Very appropriate. They consider us in the same category as rats."

Dark had been standing, casually at ease, before the Chief's desk, with the air of a man who does not tire from standing. Now he did something Fancher would not have dared: without the Chief's invitation, Dark sat down in a comfortable chair, leaned back and stretched out his legs in relaxation.

"It's a little hard for me to realize there's a twenty-five-year gap in my memory," he said. "It seems to me that it has been less than a month ago that Goat and I were together, with other refugees from the government edict, in the Icaria Desert. Why did you ask me about Goat?"

"Because the government brought him back to Mars City not three months ago," answered the Chief. "None of us had any idea where he was, but it turns out that the government has had him working under surveillance some place in the Xanthe Desert north of Solis Lacus. Since it was not far from Solis Lacus that you were picked up, I wondered if you had had any contact with him."

"Not that I remember," said Dark. "Do you have another of those cigars?"

"Why, yes," answered the Chief, startled. He produced another Hadriacum cigar and handed it to Dark. Dark lit it and puffed the fragrant smoke with evident enjoyment.

"As I say, the last time I remember seeing Goat was in the Icaria Desert, in a dome we had set up there," said Dark. "The next thing I remember is waking up in the midst of some sort of cave in a different part of Icaria, surrounded by Martians.

"I could communicate with them in a fashion—something I was never able to do before—and they were able to write the name of the Childress Barber College so I could read it. But they evidently don't differentiate our dome cities by name. I had no idea the college was here in Mars City until your men contacted me; I just assumed it was at Solis Lacus."

"You'd have waged a merry search for it, clear on the other side of Mars," remarked the Chief. "What was your purpose in finding it?"

"I don't know that I had any specific purpose," replied Dark easily. "I gathered from the Martians that here I could find someone who concurred with my philosophy of resisting the government edict against seeking self-sufficiency on Mars, and this was more or less confirmed by your two men who contacted me at Solis Lacus."

"I'll see to it that in the future they're not quite so frank until they're sure of their man," said the Chief darkly. He looked quizzically at Fancher, and Fancher nodded slightly. "But it's true. As a matter of fact, the Phoenix follows the path toward self-sufficiency that you recommended, rather than the one sought by Goat Hennessey."

"That's the wrong way to approach it," said Dark promptly. "Goat and the other scientists were following a line offering valid possibilities in their genetic research. The only reason the rest of us chose to attempt the extrasensory powers–particularly teleportation–was that we were not qualified in genetic research and this seemed a field in which we stood a chance to contribute along alternate lines. The effort should be followed along both lines."

"The government managed to capture all the scientists at the time of your disappearance, and it was assumed that you had been captured, too," said the Chief. "We don't have any scientists in the Phoenix who are capable of doing Goat Hennessey's type of research."

"You say he's in Mars City? I wonder if it would do any good for me to contact him."

"I told you that he was the one who betrayed the whole thing to the government, and he's been working under government supervision these last twenty-five years. I wouldn't trust him."

The Chief surveyed Dark's strong face with speculative green eyes, then added:

"As a matter of fact, we've made a certain amount of progress following your line of research. Since there are probably a good many things you discovered in this work that we haven't stumbled on yet, we could use your help in developing it, if you're interested."

"Very definitely," answered Dark. "I'm interested in seeing what you've done, and I'll be glad to help in any way I can."

"There's one thing," said the Chief, measuring his words. "I've held this organization together despite some pretty severe reverses for more than fifteen years now. The reason I've been able to do it is that I expect and must insist on absolute obedience to my orders."

Dark smiled. "I said that I would be willing to help you," he replied gently. "I follow no man's orders."

The green eyes fixed themselves unwinkingly on the pale-blue ones for a long moment. The blue ones did not waver.

At last, to Fancher's utter amazement, the Chief nodded agreement.

5

Maya Cara Nome looked from her furnished room through cracked shutters at the building across the street.

A barber college. The building at 49 Sage Avenue, Mars City, was a barber college.

That surprised her. She didn't know exactly what she had expected: a hospital, perhaps, or even a kindergarten. But a barber college!

But the source of the information she had received that 49 Sage Avenue was the address she sought was unimpeachable. She had ferreted it out, after a long time and through devious ways, and she was sure she could trust it.

"The Childress Barber College" read the neatly lettered sign above the door. Maya's landlady, moon-faced Mrs. Chan, had pointed out Oxvane Childress to her as he left the building one day: a big man, comfortably stomached, with a heavy brown beard which, even at that distance, she could see was shot with gray.

As innocent as you please. Childress came out and went in, the students went in and came out. Still, it was the address she had been given.

Maya had to gain entrance to the building. She could learn nothing watching it from outside. She was established here as a tourist from Earth; besides, the position and activities of women were prescribed rigidly by Martian colonial convention, and women did not study to become barbers on Mars.

She would have to have help. She, thought at once of Nuwell, and as immediately rejected him.

"Maya, I don't see why you insist on working alone," he had complained. "I can set the whole machinery of government in motion to help you, whenever you need it." "Primarily because you're well known and your activities are observed," she had answered. "Your whole government machinery hasn't been effective in tracking down the rebel headquarters yet, and it's reasonable to assume that the rebels have a fairly effective intelligence network. My job is to find that headquarters, and if I were seen very often with you or tried to utilize your government machinery, they'd have me pinpointed pretty soon."

She left the window, filled a tiny basin with precious water, shrugged out of her negligee and sponged her small, perfect body. She donned form-fitting tunic, briefs and short skirt, pulled on knee-length socks and laced up Martian walking shoes. She spent some time preparing her hair and face.

Then she left the room and the house and walked uptown. The walk was about a kilometer, along sidewalks bordered by cubical, functional houses and trim lawns of terrestrial grass and small trees. Above the city, its dome was opalescent in the morning sun.

The small houses gave way to larger business buildings, also cubical, and the lawns dwindled and vanished. Farther down, the buildings were even larger and the streets were wider and busier; but she was not going into the heart of Mars City.

She turned into an office building, and studied the directory in the lobby. The offices were those of doctors and lawyers. On the directory she found "Charlworth Scion, Attorney-at-Law, Room 207."

There was no elevator. Maya walked up the stairs and down a corridor, finding a door that had nothing on it but the number. She turned the knob and went in.

The small outer office was uninhabited. It was carpeted and desked, with two straight chairs against a wall, for clients. Through a door, she could see part of the inner office, cluttered and stacked with papers and books. She stood there, hesitating. The outer door clicked shut behind her. At the sound, a gray-haired, preoccupied man with spectacles and stooped shoulders peered from the inner office.

"Oh!" he said. "I'm sorry, my secretary went to lunch a bit early today. Can I help you, Miss?"

"I'm looking for Mr. Scion," she said.

"I'm Charlworth Scion."

"Terra outshines the Sun," said Maya.

Scion's eyes were suddenly wary behind the spectacles.

"Well, well," he murmured. "Come in, please."

She went into the cluttered inner office, and Scion closed and locked the door.

"And you are ...?" said Scion behind his desk, his pale hands fumbling aimlessly with papers.

"Maya Cara Nome," she said.

Scion found a paper and scanned it. He apparently found her name there.

"I'm surprised to see you here," he admitted. "Our information was that you would be working entirely alone."

"I am," said Maya. "Or I was. I was told not to contact you unless I had to, Mr. Scion, but it seems I'm going to need some help."

Scion inclined his head, but said nothing.

"As you may or may not know, my specific assignment is to locate the nerve center of rebellious activity," said Maya. "It seems that the rebels have an intelligence network about as effective as the government's, and it was felt that a woman tourist from Earth might be successful where any unusual probing by local agents might arouse suspicion."

"That's true," conceded Scion. "I doubt that they're really sure of the identity of more than a few of our agents, but sometimes I think they have a card file on every person on Mars. We have to be very careful that movements of our agents are consistent with their pretended occupations."

"I have a reliable tip that their nerve center is the Childress Barber College here," she said. "I can't find out anything, though, unless I get into the building over a period of time. As a woman, I can't very well apply to study barbering."

"No," said Scion. "I see your problem."

He turned to a filing cabinet, unlocked it and searched through it, whistling tunelessly. He found a folder, pulled it out and studied it.

"If it is, they've certainly kept it well covered," he said. "There's not a mark of suspicion entered against the Childress Barber College. But here's a possibility for getting you in. The barber college employs one secretary, female. Now, if you could take her place...."

Maya smiled.

"I might as well apply as a barber student," she said. "You propose to remove a trusted member of their own group from their midst and replace her with a complete unknown?"

"We don't know that she's a rebel," answered Scion. "If she isn't, she can be lured away to another job at a much better salary. If she is, and can't be lured ... well, there are other methods. The Mars City Employment Agency is operated by one of our agents, and you'll be the only secretary available when the barber college asks for a woman to fill her place.

"Believe me, Miss Cara Nome, as easy as it is for a woman to get married on Mars, it is difficult to find women to do any sort of business work. It won't seem at all strange that you're the only one available."

"The only trouble is that I'm known in the neighborhood as a tourist from Earth," objected Maya.

"Well," said Scion, "things have been more expensive than you planned for on Mars. You've run short of money.

You have to work for a while to pay living expenses here until the next ship leaves for Earth."

"My account at the bank?"

"It will vanish quietly from the records," said Scion with a smile. "The bank is a government institution."

"Very well," said Maya, taking her purse from his desk. "Let me know when I'm to apply."

"You won't hear from me again," said Scion, shaking his head. "The employment agency will notify you to appear at the barber college for an interview."

Maya knew of Scion only as her emergency contact on Mars. She did not know what position he held in that underground network of terrestrial agents which was largely unknown even to Nuwell Eli, the government prosecutor. But, whatever his position, he got things done in a hurry.

Within two weeks, Maya was typing up applications, examination reports and supply orders in the Childress Barber College, joking and flirting with barber students between classes, and naively declaiming to her ostensible employer, phlegmatic Oxvane Childress, how lucky it was for her that she was able to get a job right across the street from her rooming house.

"The work's easy," rumbled Childress, explaining her tasks to her. "Any time you want to take a coffee break with any of the young men, or go uptown shopping, go ahead, as long as the work gets done. Just one thing: you have to stay up here in the front of the building, and don't ever go back in the classrooms. The instructors are mighty strict about that, and that's one rule I won't stand to be violated."

This significant restriction convinced Maya she was on the right track. But she needed to move cautiously, if she was not to arouse immediate suspicion. So she adhered strictly to her role for nearly a month, keeping her eyes open.

If it was a rebel operation, it was almost perfectly disguised. Childress performed the duties of the administrative head of a barber college, and nothing more. The students, about fifty of them, went in and out at regular school hours, and she became casually acquainted with a good many of them. The half-dozen instructors, whom she also came to know, were less regular in their movements, but she could detect nothing suspicious about them.

"We cut the hair of Mars," was the college's motto, and she learned that it was the larger of only two barber colleges on the planet. Apparently, it actually did supply graduate barbers to all the dome cities. It took in customers for the students to practice on, and, although many of them were strangers, some of them were prominent Mars City citizens whom she knew by sight.

There was no question about it: partially, at least, it was a legitimate barber college, whatever other activities it might mask. The only thing noticeably unusual on the surface was that it was extremely selective in its approval of students who applied for courses in barbering. She discerned that through her processing of the applications.

If she was going to find out anything definite, she would have to get into the forbidden rear portion of the building. But obviously there were legitimate classrooms there, in addition to the activities she suspected, and if she were caught nosing around the classrooms she would be discharged at once for violation of the rules, without finding out what she sought. She would have to hit it right the first time.

Biding her time and watching, she was able to learn, almost intuitively, from the movements of students, customers and instructors, that the classrooms in which barbering was actually taught were all concentrated on the western side of the building. If there were any more sinister activities, they occurred on the opposite side. Having determined this, she planned her course of action.

Near the end of her first month at work, she chose her time one day when Childress was downtown, leaving her alone in the business office. The afternoon classes were in full swing.

Taking along a filled-out order form as an excuse, Maya walked quickly down the corridor that stretched across the front of the building. Carefully and quietly, she pushed open the door at the extreme end of the corridor—a little surprised, as a matter of fact, to find it unlocked.

She was in another corridor, that struck straight back to the rear of the building.

She hesitated. There were doors spaced all along both sides of this corridor. Did she dare attempt to open one, on the chance that the room behind it was unoccupied?

Then she saw that one door, a little way down, stood half open. Quietly she walked down the hall, not quite to the door, but near enough to it to be able to see a large area of the room behind it.

There were people in there. In the part she was able to see, there were half a dozen students seated, and one of the instructors standing among them. Fortunately, their backs were to her.

Whatever they were studying, it was not barbering. There was an occasional murmur of voices, but she could not make out the words.

Then she saw! On the table at the front of the room, which the students faced, there was a big barber's basin.

As she watched, the basin slowly raised off the table and moved upward a few inches. No one was near it, but it floated there, quivering and tilting a little, in the air. And then, from it, slowly, the water itself came up in a weird fountain, moved completely free of the basin and hung above it in the air, gradually assuming the form of a globe.

Telekinesis! This was a class in telekinesis! The students were concentrating on the basin and water, and lifting them into the air by the power of their minds.

This was indeed the heart of the rebel movement. She had found what she sought.

"Aren't you where you shouldn't be, young lady?" asked a calm masculine voice behind her.

Shocked, terrified, she whirled. A tall, handsome, dark-haired man she had never seen before was standing there, observing her quizzically. His pale eyes seemed to look through her and beyond her.

She forced herself to casual composure.

"I don't believe I've met you," she said. "Are you one of the instructors?"

"I'm Dark Kensington, one of the supervisors," he replied. "And you're Miss Cara Nome, the secretary, who shouldn't be back here."

Had he noticed that she saw the telekinetic action? She glanced back at the classroom. The basin was now comfortably ensconced back on the table, full of water.

"I had this order, which I thought was of an emergency nature," she said, offering it to him. "Mr. Childress wasn't in, and I thought I'd better find one of the instructors so it could be approved and go out right away."

Dark took it and glanced at it.

"I doubt that its emergency nature is as grave as you may have thought," he said soberly. "However, Mr. Childress would be better qualified to judge that. You understand that I shall have to report this infraction of the rules to him."

Suddenly, Maya was overwhelmed by an utterly terrifying sensation. It seemed that these pale-blue eyes were looking into her mind, searching, seeking to determine her thoughts and her true intention.

Instinctively, not knowing how she did it, she veiled her thoughts with a psychic barrier. And, instinctively, she recognized that he detected the barrier and could not penetrate it.

Telepathy? Why not, if they were experimenting successfully with telekinesis?

"I'm sorry," she murmured hurriedly, and brushed past him. He did not try to detain her.

She hurried back to the office. She hurried, but as she hurried down first the one corridor and then the other, she discovered that her steps were slowing involuntarily. A powerful force seemed to be detaining her, attempting to draw her back.

Frightened but curious, she attempted to analyze this force even as she struggled against it. She could not be sure–it was disturbing, either way, but she could not be sure whether it was a telepathic thing or merely the magnetic force of this man's powerful masculine personality that pulled at her.

In a state of mental turmoil, she reached the office. Childress was not yet back.

Should she wait for him?

Then, as suddenly as she had sensed Dark Kensington's telepathic probing, she sensed something else. Somewhere in the back of the building, he was talking to another man she had not seen before, and within ten minutes Dark Kensington would be in this office. And the prospect she faced was far more serious than mere discharge for infringement of company rules.

She had to get in touch with Nuwell at once. She recognized that if she could get out of this building and across the street to her rooming house, she would be safe for a little while. She could telephone Nuwell from there.

Grabbing her purse, she hastened out of the office.

6

The three men who stood by a table in the back lobby of the Childress Barber College and checked off the departure of the men at regularly spaced intervals were as different in appearance as they were in their positions in the Order of the Phoenix.

Oxvane Childress, big and bearded, was the "front," and directed the very necessary task of administering the Childress Barber College as a genuine barber college. Childress was a prominent member of two of Mars City's civic and social clubs, and careful examination of his activities over a period of years would have thrown no suspicion on him.

The Chief, whose real name perhaps Childress knew but never spoke, was a huge-headed midget who directed the far-flung activities of the Order of the Phoenix as an underground rebel organization. He never left the building, but reports were brought in to him from all over Mars. He knew a great deal at any time about what the government and Marscorp were doing, and he gave the orders for those moves aimed at maintaining the secrecy of the Phoenix.

Dark Kensington, tall and pale-eyed, had moved at once into the natural position of guiding the experimental work of the organization in extrasensory perception and telekinesis. He was able to add his knowledge of earlier work to the progress that had been made since his disappearance, and co-ordinated the studies in the various dome cities.

A little behind the three stood Fancher Laddigan, doing the actual checking with a pencil on a list in his hand.

"I think it's all unnecessary," rumbled Childress unhappily. "I watched the girl carefully while she was here, and the usual checks were made into her background. It's true she had some social contacts with Nuwell Eli when she first came to Mars, but there's nothing sinister about that association and it seems the last thing a Marscorp agent would do openly. As far as I could determine, she just realized she'd violated a rule and would be discharged for it, so she left before she could be discharged."

"She hasn't returned to her rooming house," remarked the Chief in his high, thin voice.

"Looking for another job, or maybe just on a trip," said Childress. "After all, she's a terrestrial tourist. If this is all a false alarm, how am I going to explain suspending operation of the college for a period?"

"Remodeling," replied the Chief. "Work out the details and put a sign up as soon as evacuation has progressed far enough."

"It may be unnecessary, Oxvane," said Dark, "but it's best not to take chances. This telepathy is a very uncertain thing, and sometimes it's hard to differentiate true telepathic communication from one's own hopes or fears. But it seemed to me that I had the very definite sense that Miss Cara Nome was seeking something with hostile intent, and it's entirely possible that she saw part of one of the experiments through that open door."

Two students appeared, gave their names to Fancher in an undertone, and sauntered out the back door of the building.

"What's the status now?" asked the Chief.

"They were nineteen and twenty," answered Fancher precisely. "They're part of Group C, which is going to Hesperidum. Group A goes to Regina, Group B to Charax, Group D to Nuba and Group E to Ismenius."

"None to Solis?" asked Childress in surprise.

"No, sir, nor to Phoenicis, either," answered Fancher. "They're both so far, and Solis is a resort, where they might be easier to detect. We're using both public transport and private groundcars. All of them so far have reported safely through the flower shop, except these last two, so the government evidently hasn't thrown a ring around the building yet."

"And I don't think they will, either," growled Childress. "I tell you, it's all unnecessary."

"Are things going smoothly here?" asked the Chief.

"Yes, sir," replied Fancher. "The last five men scheduled to leave are taking care of any customers who come in, and the rest of them are packing supplies into the trucks. As soon as I get word from the flower shop that the last pair has cleared, I give another pair the word to leave."

"It seems to be moving along well," said the Chief, and he turned his green eyes upon Childress. "Is the business office manned?"

"Why—why, there's no one there right now," said Childress, taken aback.

"I think it would look extremely peculiar to any investigator if you weren't there, frantically trying to locate a new secretary," said the Chief quietly.

Childress left, in confusion. The Chief turned to Dark.

"I think Fancher's handling this very well without my help," he said. "You know where your groundcar is, if we all have to make a run for it?"

"Yes," answered Dark. "We won't be going together?"

"No," replied the Chief, and his lips twisted in a faint smile. "I have my own method of exit, which should give them other things to think about."

He left, moving with quick, short steps. Dark stayed for a few moments more, then he too went back into the building to help with packing.

The Lowland Flower Shop, on the other side of Mars City, near the west airlock, was the clearance point for the evacuees. The flower shop was operated by a Phoenix agent, and each pair that left the barber college passed

through there before leaving the city to let those behind
know that they had not been stopped by government
men. Other Phoenix agents watched the heliport and bus
station for any evidence that the government was trying
to block these routes out of Mars City.

The evacuation moved steadily, and it began to
appear that Childress was right. Singly, the first two of
the five trucks moved out, and all of the ESP instructors
and thirty-two of the students had reported back safe
clearance from the flower shop, when....

Dark was moving a stack of charts from one of the
classrooms to the basement when bells all over the
building set up a tremendous clangor. Immediately the
quiet evacuation dissolved into an uproar, with men
running and shouting and the bell ringing incessantly.

Dark knew what had happened. Childress, in the
front office, had seen government agents approaching, or
perhaps they had actually entered the building. He had
pressed the alarm bell, then sought to delay them with
the righteous indignation suitable to the administrative
head of a barber college which is invaded by government
officials.

The bells stopped suddenly, and the scattered
shouting sounded strange and thin in the comparative
silence. Then the piping voice of the Chief came over the
loudspeakers spread throughout the building.

"Attention!" said the Chief. "We are temporarily safe.
The alarm automatically sealed all doors to the building
behind the front corridor.

"Kensington, please come to my office. The rest of you,
tie up the customers still here and leave them unharmed,
and then leave the building by the emergency exits.
Scatter, and make your way by whatever private
transportation methods you can to the rendezvous
assigned to your respective group. Do not use public
transportation, because Marscorp will undoubtedly be
checking public transport now."

Dark set the charts down on the stairs and made his way back to the Chief's office. The Chief was sitting, tiny behind his big desk, his face as serene as ever. He was puffing casually on one of the long Hadriacum cigars. Dark laughed.

"You don't have another of those cigars, do you?" he asked.

For the first time since he had been here, Dark saw the Chief's mouth break into a full, broad smile.

"I think so," said the Chief, an undertone of delight bubbling in his voice. He reached into the desk and pulled one out. Dark accepted it gravely, and lit it.

"The last two evacuees haven't reported to the flower shop, and they're overdue," said the Chief, his face getting serious. "Childress hasn't reported back here by telephone, either, so the Marscorp gang probably had already entered the building before he detected them and sounded the alarm."

"What about Childress?" asked Dark. "What will happen to him?"

"He'll take the rap," answered the Chief. "His defense will be that if there were any Phoenix activities going on here he didn't know about it. He was just running a barber college in good faith. I don't think they can prove otherwise."

"Do we have any idea what our situation is?" asked Dark.

"A very accurate idea. We have observers posted in the two houses at the ends of our emergency exits, and they've been reporting to Fancher, in the next room, by telephone. There's a force of about a hundred Mars City policemen and plain-clothes agents in the streets all around the building. They saw a squad go into the front, but evidently they didn't have enough warning to let Childress know in time."

"Will the doors hold?"

The Chief's mouth quirked.

"They'll need demolition equipment to break them down," he said. "All these have are heatguns and tear gas. One of the observers farther downtown said he saw a tank heading this way, but if they don't already know there are innocent customers in here, Childress will tell them."

"Then everybody gets away but Childress?"

"We hope. They're not going to ignore these surrounding houses, especially with men drifting out of them and moving away. That's why I want to stress the importance of one thing to you, Kensington: you're too important for us to lose at this juncture, with your knowledge of the original work done. That house at the end of your exit will have a dozen or so of our men in it, waiting to drift away one by one, but you can't afford to worry about them. I want you to get in that groundcar, alone, and take off like Phobos rising."

"You're going out the other emergency exit?"

"That's none of your business. But, as a matter of fact, no. If you want to see something that will throw consternation into this Marscorp outfit, watch the roof of this building. Now, get moving, Kensington, and good luck. Fancher and I will be leaving as soon as he gets all the records packed."

The Chief held out his tiny hand, and Dark shook hands with him. Then Dark left, went down into the basement and entered an underground door in its eastern wall. He had to crawl through the tunnel driven through the sand under the street.

He emerged in the basement of a house across the street, which ostensibly was owned by Manfall Kingron, a retired space engineer. He went upstairs.

About half the personnel of the barber college who had not been caught by the alarm were roaming the rooms of the small house, drifting singly out the back door at ten-minute intervals.

Dark went to the front window and looked across the street at the barber college.

The street was full of men carrying heat pistols, moving restlessly, facing the barber college. Some of them were in police uniform. Squads of them moved about on the college grounds, and a few were in the yards of houses on this side of the street.

Dark watched the roof.

As he did so, from its center a helicopter rose into the air, hovering over the building, moving upward slowly.

So that was the Chief's escape method. He had smuggled a helicopter into the domed city itself! But how was he to get out of the city in it?

The appearance of the copter threw the men outside into confused excitement. They ran about, aiming their short-range heat beams futilely up at the rising copter.

A military tank, undoubtedly the one the Chief had been told about, spun around the corner. It stopped, and its guns swung upward toward the copter. But they remained silent. Heavy heat beams or artillery could puncture the city's protecting dome.

The copter went straight up, gathering speed. Up, and up, and it did not stop!

It hit the plastic dome near its zenith. It tilted and staggered. It ripped through the dome and vanished.

Immediately, sirens began to wail throughout the city. Doors clanged shut automatically everywhere. Lights and warning signs flashed at every street corner, advising citizens to run for the nearest airtight shelter.

The dome was punctured!

Emergency crews would be up within minutes to repair the break, and very little of the city's air would hiss away. But, in the meantime, every activity in Mars City was snarled by the necessity to seek shelter. The Chief had, indeed, created a situation of consternation in which it would be easier for the Phoenix men to elude their enemies.

The armed men of the government forces were already running for the houses in this area. Some of them were headed for the house from which Dark watched. The Phoenix men were donning marsuits. They would admit the refugees, after requiring them to lay down their arms, and then leave the house in their marsuits. Dark grinned happily, and walked quickly through the house to the attached garage. He climbed into the groundcar, started the engine, and opened the garage door by the remote control mechanism on the dashboard.

Accelerating at full power, Dark drove the groundcar out of the garage and spun into the street. The men afoot, seeking entrance to the houses, paid no attention. The tank began to turn ponderously in his direction, but by the time it was in a position to bring its guns to bear, Dark's groundcar had reached the corner and raced around it into the broad thoroughfare leading to Mars City's east airlock.

The airlock was only a dozen blocks away. The Chief's theory had been that the government, depending on surprise in its move to surround the Childress Barber College, would not attempt the complicated task of checking all traffic passing through the airlock until it was realized that some of the Phoenix men had escaped from the trap at the college.

Dark reached the airlock in minutes. The Chief's theory proved correct. There were no police at the airlock, and the maintenance employee stationed there did not even look up as Dark's approach activated the inner door.

He drove the groundcar into the airlock. The inner door closed behind him. The outer door opened, and Dark drove out onto the highway that struck straight across the Syrtis Major Lowland toward the Aeria Desert and Edom. It was as simple as that.

About ten miles out was the circular bypass highway that surrounded Mars City, and Dark proposed to turn right on that, for his destination was Hesperidum. The highway he was on would take him eastward, and

Hesperidum was about 8,000 kilometers southwest of Mars City—a little better than two-days' drive at groundcar speed on the straight, flat highways. Dark reached over and set the groundcar's radio dial on the frequency which had been agreed on for emergency Phoenix broadcasts during this operation. If government monitors caught the broadcasts and jammed them, there were alternate channels chosen. With only about two dozen radio stations on all Mars, plus the official aircraft and groundcar band, there was plenty of free room in the air.

There was nothing on the Phoenix frequency now but a little disconsolate static.

The country through which he drove here was uninhabited lowland. The human life on Mars, agricultural, industrial and commercial, was concentrated under the domes of the cities. Except for a few tiny individual domes at the edge of Mars City, there were no human structures close to it except the airport and the spaceport, and these were west and north of the city, respectively.

The highway struck straight and lonely through a faintly rippling sea of gray-green canal sage, spotted occasionally with the tall trunk of a canal cactus, rising above it. Later he would see infrequent dome farms, but he could expect no more than two or three score of these in the entire long drive to Hesperidum.

Dark slowed and entered the cloverleaf that took him onto the bypass expressway. Even as he did so, the radio crackled and the thin voice of the Chief sounded over the groundcar loudspeaker.

"Attention, Phoenix," said the Chief intensely. "Attention, Phoenix. Emergency instructions. We have monitored reports that the government is checking airlocks at all cities. Repeat: the government is checking airlocks at all cities.

"Some Phoenix have been captured attempting to leave Mars City. Instructions: those in Mars City do not attempt to leave but find shelter with Phoenix friends. Those beyond dome without credentials, go to assigned emergency rendezvous spots *outside* dome cities. Repeat instructions: those...."

Swearing under his breath, Dark pulled the groundcar to a stop beside the highway. It was so simple! They should have foreseen that the government would take such a step as soon as it was realized that the Phoenix men were leaving Mars City. He himself evidently had gotten through the airlock just in time.

But he had been assigned no outside rendezvous! Whether it was an oversight or not, he did not know, but the only place he had been instructed to go was Hesperidum. The only Phoenix contact he knew was the South Ausonia Art Shop in Hesperidum; and now he could not enter the city without being captured.

He had only one alternative: the Martians, in the Icaria Desert, halfway around Mars. They would remember him and shelter him, and he was sure he could find the spot.

He looked at his fuel gauge. The tank was full. It would not take him quite there, but he could chance refueling at Solis Lacus, some 20,000 kilometers from Mars City. He could take the highway, turning out into the desert to go around Edom, Aram and Ophir.

He put the groundcar in drive again, and made a U-turn in the highway. He entered the cloverleaf and was halfway through it when he saw the copter.

It was a red-and-white government copter, and it was descending at a shallow angle toward him from the direction of Mars City. Dark switched his radio to the official channel.

" ... await check. Repeat: groundcar in cloverleaf, stop at once and await check."

Dark braked the groundcar to a stop. As soon as the copter grounded, he could accelerate and escape.

But the copter did not ground. It hovered, directly over him. Then Dark realized it was awaiting a patrol car from Mars City to check and take him in custody if necessary.

Immediately, he put the groundcar in drive and whipped out of the cloverleaf under full acceleration. If he could only achieve top speed, 350 kilometers-an-hour, the copter couldn't match it.

But the copter was on his tail at once as he swerved out of the tight curve. Its guns spat fire.

There was a terrific impact, and the groundcar dome shattered above him. Unprotected, he felt the air explode from the groundcar, from his lungs. Oxygenless death poured in through the broken dome.

It all happened in an instant. Even as the dome shattered under the copter's shell and Dark recognized the imminence of death, the groundcar twisted out of control and careened from the highway. He felt it spinning over and over, and then blackness closed in around him.

7

Maya had never seen Nuwell in such a state of sustained rage.

He strode back and forth in the private dining room of the Syrtis Major Club, near the western edge of Mars City, slapping his fist into his hand. His face usually was engaging and boyish, the wave of his dark hair setting it off handsomely, but now it was flushed like that of a petulant child and the lock of hair hung down over his forehead. Maya, the only other person in the room, sat quietly and watched him pace.

"They had plenty of time and all the information they needed," stormed Nuwell, "and yet they didn't get a single one of the key men! Most of the rebels slipped out easily, right under their noses!"

Maya watched him detachedly. This was the man she had promised to marry, and, as she had once or twice before, she was undergoing pangs of doubt. After all, she had known Nuwell Eli only during the few months she had been on Mars.

She had fallen in love with him for his charm, his intelligence, his good-humored gentleness, but she did not like this display of temper. It was not a controlled anger, but had something of the irrational in it.

"Childress was captured," she reminded him.

"Childress! A figurehead! He says he didn't know about the rebel activities going on in the college, and he's so stupid I may not be able to make a case against him."

Maya recognized that this element, the success of his prosecution, was a very important factor to Nuwell.

"Are the twelve I identified the only ones captured?" asked Maya.

"Yes. Twelve captured, seven killed, and every one of them small fry. The leaders undoubtedly got away in that copter. We blockaded the airlocks fast, so most of the others are probably still in the city, but we don't have any idea where to look for them."

"I may be able to help in that, when I get back from my swing around the other cities," said Maya.

"I don't want you to go on that jaunt, Maya!" exclaimed Nuwell, swinging around to face her with fierce emphasis. "You said when you had found the headquarters, you'd resign the service and marry me. Now you want to go all over Mars looking for rebels!"

"Nuwell, I can identify almost all of those who were at the barber college," Maya remonstrated. "They've picked up some men at the airlocks and others on the roads at several cities, and even Martian law won't permit you to uproot those people and send them to Mars City just on suspicion. They can't be sent here for me to identify: I'll have to go there."

"We can work out some charges to get them extradited to Mars City," snapped Nuwell angrily. "I don't want you to go, Maya. I want you to stay here and marry me, immediately."

"Aren't you being a little dictatorial, Nuwell?" she suggested coolly.

The warning implied in her remoteness seemed to trigger a polarized reaction in Nuwell. The furious dark eyes melted suddenly, the stubborn anger of the face altered on the instant to a sentimental, wistful smile of appeal.

"Don't be angry, Maya," he pleaded, half-ruefully, half-humorously. "It's just that I love you so much. It's just that I'm impatient for you to be my wife."

Changeability is attributed to the feminine, but Maya was not able to shift her mood as facilely as her fiance.

"If I'm worth marrying, I'm worth waiting for a little longer," she said, with an edge to her voice. She was angry at Nuwell for acting so like a spoiled child. "I'm

going to see this job finished. I'm leaving for Solis Lacus
on the jetliner tonight."

"Solis Lacus!" he exclaimed in astonishment. "Why,
Maya, that's halfway around Mars!"

"That's exactly why the rebels might be more likely to
go there. In spite of the patrols, you know they haven't
picked up all of the rebels who escaped Mars City by
groundcar. Any of them who headed for Solis Lacus will
be arriving there within the next two or three days. Then
I'll make a swing around and spend as much time as
necessary at each of the dome cities before coming back
here."

The angry, stubborn expression swept across Nuwell's
face again.

"Maya, I won't–" he began.

But at that moment, their guests began arriving. As
the judge of Mars City's superior court and his wife
entered the room, Nuwell cut himself off sharp and
turned to greet them. His face cleared instantly, his lips
curved into a delighted smile and he welcomed them with
such natural, innocent charm that one would have
thought he was incapable of frowning.

The presence of the guests seemed to intoxicate him
with good-humor, and when he had to leave in the midst
of the party to drive Maya to the airport he did not
resume his argument. He merely kissed her good-bye
tenderly before she boarded the plane and begged her
with melting eyes to hurry back because he would be
lonely every moment she was away.

So it was that Maya stretched in a reclining chair on
the sundeck of the Chateau Nectaris the next afternoon
and permitted herself to be disgusted with the entire
planet Mars.

Maya's small, perfect body was kept minimally
modest by one of those scanty Martian sunsuits. A huge
straw hat, woven of dried canal sage, hid her beautiful
face.

A disappointing resort area for an Earthwoman, this Solis Lacus Lowland. No swimming, no boating, no skiing. No water and no snow. Just a vast expanse of salty ground, blanketed with gray-green canal sage and dotted with the plastic domes of the resort chateaus. Nothing to do but hike in a marsuit or sun oneself under a dome.

She had chosen the Chateau Nectaris because it was the largest of the resort spots, and therefore the most likely one to be chosen by men who sought to hide out for a while. She had contacted the managers of all the resort chateaus and all had agreed to let her know of the arrival of any new guests.

There had been three of them during the morning, two arriving by groundcar and one by copter, at three different chateaus. She had driven to each one and circumspectly inspected the new guest, but none had been anyone she recognized from the Childress Barber College.

In a way, she wished she had yielded to Nuwell's importunities. There was much more of interest to do in Mars City. And Nuwell *was* charming and intelligent and rather dashing, and she did love him, and she did want to marry him. But....

But she was right in wanting to help identify those rebels who had been captured before she considered her task finished. And perhaps Nuwell had been right in his implied disagreement with her idea of coming first to Solis Lacus, so far from Mars City. Logically, would it not be harder to lose oneself in a fashionable resort area than in a good-sized city? But something within her had urged her to come here first. It was a hunch, and she intended to play it.

With a sigh, Maya pushed the hat off her face and stared with exotically slanted black eyes at the shining blur of the dome hundreds of feet above her. She sat up, hugging her knees with her arms.

A score of other guests were sunning themselves here also. At her movement, the unmarried men turned their eyes on her frankly; the married ones did so furtively, to be promptly yanked back to attention by their wives.

Maya's onyx eyes surveyed this dullness aloofly, then lifted over the nearby parapet and across the sparse terrestrial lawn which would grow only under the dome. The far cliffs of the Thaumasia Foelix Desert loomed darkly, distorted through the dome's sides.

The dome's airlock opened to admit a groundcar. She watched it, interestedly, as it scurried like a huge, glassy bug along the curving road and disappeared under the parapet in front of the chateau. Mail from Mars City, perhaps, or supplies. Maybe even a new guest.

Something struck her, now that the groundcar was no longer in sight. It had been a little too far away to discern its details clearly, but there was something strange about the appearance of that groundcar. A glassy bug, but not entirely sleek and shiny. Rather like a bug that had come out second best in an argument with another bug.

Maya arose, purposefully. She stretched lithely, to the delight of the assembled viewers, and padded gracefully toward the chateau's second-floor entrance, trailing the huge hat in one hand.

She walked lightly along the balcony over the lobby, toward her room. As she turned its corner, passing the grand stairway, she could see the chateau entrance and the registration desk.

The groundcar had brought a new guest. He was signing the registration book, a tall, broad-shouldered man in a marsuit, holding his marshelmet under his arm. Why would he be wearing a marsuit in a groundcar?

As she looked, he laid down the pen and turned. His face was darkly tanned, strong, handsome. His hair was black as midnight, his eyes startlingly pale in the dark face.

His gaze lifted to the balcony, and Maya ducked behind the big hat just in time.

Dark Kensington!

Triumph swept through her. She had been right in coming here! This was Dark Kensington, the man she had met once, just before the raid on the college. This was one of the leaders!

The hat held casually to conceal her face, Maya walked on to her room.

The telephone was ringing as she entered. She dropped the hat on the bed, and answered it.

"Miss Cara Nome, this is Quelman Gren, the manager," said the male voice on the line. "You asked me to notify you about any new guests. One has just registered."

"I saw him," she said. "What can you tell me about him?"

"He is registered as D. Kensington, from Hesperidum," answered Gren. "He is just staying overnight. His groundcar dome was broken in an accident, and he wants to have it replaced and the groundcar refueled."

"Thank you," said Maya. "Now, please put in a call for me to S. Nuwell Eli in Mars City."

She had bathed and dressed for dinner by the time the call came through.

"Nuwell," she said, when he had identified himself on the other end of the line, "I knew I was right in coming here. One of the rebel leaders just registered."

"Are you sure?" he asked excitedly.

"Certainly I am. He was one of those who stayed hidden in the back of the barber college, and I saw him for the first time the day of the raid. He identified himself then as a supervisor. But he's just staying overnight."

"That's long enough! I'll get a jet and be up in a few hours. Get the police to take him in custody and hold him for me."

"Darling, there aren't any police at Solis Lacus," Maya reminded him. "This is a private resort area. The nearest police are at Ophir."

There was a silence while Nuwell digested this.

"You say he's staying overnight?" Nuwell said then. "I can be there before midnight with some men to take him in custody."

"I'm a trained agent," said Maya. "I can take him in custody for you."

"You'll do no such thing!" squawked Nuwell in alarm. "It's, too dangerous! Now you listen to me, Maya. You stay out of sight of this man and wait till I get there!"

"All right, darling, I'll use my own judgment," replied Maya demurely, and hung up.

She sat and cogitated for a time. She was dressed for dinner, and she had been looking forward to appearing in the dining room in the somewhat sensational moulded, flame-red gown she had bought recently in Mars City. She didn't relish the idea of having dinner sent to her room, and sitting up here alone to eat it.

With sudden decision, she arose. She donned dark glasses and tossed a powder-red veil over her dark hair. Kensington had only seen her once and would not be expecting to see her here. If he saw her now, he wouldn't recognize her.

Fifteen minutes later, she was sipping an extremely expensive martini in the dining room when she raised her eyes to see Dark Kensington enter, wearing a dark-red, form-fitting evening suit.

He paused just inside the door and stood there, slowly surveying the room. His eyes fell on Maya and paused. Then he walked straight to her table.

"May I join you, Miss Cara Nome?" he asked in a deep, controlled voice, a rather sardonic smile on his lips.

She felt trapped, and irrationally angry at him for recognizing her.

"I'm afraid you've made a mistake," she said coldly. "That isn't my name."

At this juncture, a helpful waiter appeared at Maya's elbow and asked in an appallingly distinct tone:

"Would you care for another drink, Miss Cara Nome, or do you wish to eat now?"

"An understandable mistake, since it's such a common name," said Dark, sitting down opposite her. He turned pale-blue eyes, remote and filled with light, on the waiter, and added: "She'll have another drink, and bring me one of the same."

The waiter left, and Maya removed her dark glasses to level furious black eyes at Dark.

"I could call the manager and complain that you're annoying me, you know," she said.

"You could," he agreed somberly. "You seem to be a very efficient tattletale. Or are you going to try to pretend that you weren't the one responsible for the raid on the college?"

She recognized that she was well in for it. He was not going to play a game of pretense. Well, she had tried— partly, anyway—to do as Nuwell wanted.

Very deliberately, she opened her purse, realizing that Dark was watching her closely, all his muscles tense. She took out a cigarette case and a lighter, laying them side by side on the table, and he relaxed visibly.

Maya extracted a cigarette and placed it between her lips casually. She picked up the lighter and balanced it in her hand.

"I assume that you're not armed, Mr. Kensington," she said.

He shrugged and smiled, revealing strong white teeth.

"Hardly, in this suit," he replied. "I'm glad to see you've decided to recognize me."

"I am," she said grimly. "Armed, I mean. This is not a cigarette lighter, but a very efficient and deadly heatgun. You're under arrest, Mr. Kensington, so I suppose you're having dinner with me whether you like it or not. Now, do you mind being a gentleman and lighting my cigarette, since this is not very good for the purpose?"

He looked at her face, then dropped his eyes to the lighter, still smiling.

"You'd better take my word for it," she advised. "I don't want to kill you, Mr. Kensington, but I won't hesitate. I'm an agent of the terrestrial government."

Dark shrugged again. He produced a lighter and leaned forward to light her cigarette, without a tremor.

The waiter returned with their drinks and an announcement.

"There's a telephone call for you from Mars City, Miss Cara Nome," he said.

Maya kept her eyes on Dark.

"Can you bring a telephone to the table?" she asked the waiter.

"Certainly, Miss," he replied. He left, and returned a moment later with a telephone. He set it before her and plugged it in under the table.

Juggling the lighter-gun gently in one hand, Maya picked up the phone. As soon as she answered it, her ears were assailed by Nuwell's agonized voice.

"Maya, I can't get up there tonight!" he said. "There aren't any jets here, and these idiots refuse to bring one in from Hesperidum or Cynia for me to use. I'll have to come up by groundcar."

Maya sat silent, stunned. It had not seemed too great a feat to her to hold Dark captive with her disguised heatgun when she was anticipating Nuwell's arrival within hours. But suddenly she felt like a hunter who has snared a lion in a rabbit trap.

"Maya, are you there?" demanded Nuwell querulously. "We'll spell each other at the wheel and drive up without stopping, but it will still take two and a half days to get there."

Maya took a deep breath.

"Come ahead," she said in a steady voice. "I'll have your man waiting for you when you get here."

"You'll what? But I thought you said he was only staying overnight! Maya, don't you do anything rash!"

"I'm afraid I already have," she said, a little ruefully. "I have him under arrest right now."

The noise at the other end of the line sounded like a dismayed shriek.

"You little fool!" he shrilled. "I told you not to do anything like that! How can you hold a man like that for two days, single-handed? Call in the police!"

"It seems to me that I already mentioned there aren't any around here," she reminded him patiently.

There was a long silence on the other end of the line. Then Nuwell said, with forced calm:

"I'm leaving immediately. In the name of space, Maya, be careful!"

Maya put the telephone quietly back in its cradle and looked across the table at the Tartar she had caught. Dark smiled at her, easily.

"So the reinforcements you were expecting won't get here tonight, after all," he remarked softly.

"He didn't say that at all!" she retorted, too quickly.

"There's hardly any point in trying to deceive me about it is there?" he pointed out. "I can tell a great deal from your conversation and the expression on your face, and I'd estimate that your help is going to have to come from Mars City by groundcar—a trip I've just made, so I know exactly how long it takes. Do you plan for us to spend these two nights in your room, or mine?"

She looked at him silently, stricken.

"I see our waiter returning," said Dark equably. "I trust you'll enjoy your meal as much as I'm going to enjoy mine, Miss Cara Nome."

8

The waiter unplugged the telephone and lifted it from their table.

"We're ready to order now," Maya said to him. "And please ask Mr. Gren to come in here."

A few moments after the waiter left, the manager came to their table. Quelman Gren was dark and thin-faced, with sleek, oily hair.

"When I told you I was here in an official capacity for the government, Mr. Gren, you said you would co-operate with me in every way possible," said Maya.

"Yes, Miss Cara Nome, I have made every effort to do so," replied Gren. "Is there some way I can help you now?"

"Yes, there is," she said. "This man is my prisoner, and I'm going to have to keep him in custody here for two days and a half, until help arrives from Mars City. I'd like for you to arm a couple of dependable men with heatguns and assign them to help me guard him."

Gren shook his head.

"I'm sorry, Miss Cara Nome, but none of the employees of the Chateau Nectaris was employed for that sort of work, and I'm not going to ask them to do it. What you should have is police help."

"As you know very well, there are no police nearer than Ophir," she said in an exasperated tone. "Surely, you have some semi-official officers employed in the chateau in case of trouble among the guests."

"I have a house detective, but his duties are to intervene only when some crime has been committed against a guest or against the chateau. You told me that you were seeking political rebels, and I assume that that is your charge against Mr. Kensington. My house detective has no authority to act in such cases, and I do not intend to get the chateau mixed up in these affairs.

"I've co-operated with you to the extent of giving you information you wanted, Miss Cara Nome, and I'll continue to co-operate insofar as I am not asked to do something I have no authority to do. It occurs to me that if you came here seeking rebels, you should have come equipped to handle them if you found them."

"It occurs to me that you act very much as though you were in sympathy with the rebel cause," retorted Maya angrily.

"My sympathies are not the government's affair, as long as I take no illegal actions," said Gren. "Good evening, Miss Cara Nome."

Maya gazed after him furiously as he left the dining room. Dark, sitting completely relaxed, smiled pleasantly at her.

"Please be assured," he said, "that I'm going to try to avoid injuring you in any way when I escape your custody."

"I'm not worried, because you aren't going to escape," she said. "But I appreciate the thought. You seem to be a very mild-mannered person, for...."

She stopped.

"For a rebel?" he finished for her. "I really don't know what sort of indoctrination you must have had, Maya–if I may call you Maya, and there's no point in being formal under the circumstances. The students at the barber college were all rebels, and the reports I received were that you got along nicely with most of them."

"Yes, I did. I don't suppose it should surprise me to find that rebels are human beings, too."

"Merely a matter of a difference in orientation. And a question for you to consider is, which orientation actually is correct?"

Maya did not like the direction the conversation was taking. She was relieved by the appearance of the waiter with their meals of thick, steaming steaks, with all the necessary trimmings.

"It will be a long time before we can be served anything like this by teleportation," she said, laughing.

"But, Mr. Kensington—"

"Dark, if you don't mind."

"Very well. Dark, you say that you drove here from Mars City. How did you avoid the copter patrols that were out trying to intercept the escaping rebels?"

"As a matter of fact, I didn't, and that's a very peculiar thing," he said thoughtfully. "One of them got me just outside Mars City and blasted the dome of my groundcar."

"I noticed you were wearing a marsuit when you registered here, and Gren said you were having the dome repaired."

"That's what's peculiar about it. I wasn't wearing the marsuit when the copter broke my dome. I didn't have any protection at all. The groundcar went off the road and overturned. I don't know how long I was unconscious, but it was evidently long enough for the copter to look me over, decide I was dead, and move on out of sight. What I can't understand is why I didn't asphyxiate."

"You mean that you were protected by no oxygen equipment at all?"

"None. I returned to consciousness and I was lying there with the dome broken wide open and my face bare to the Martian air. I got into my marsuit right away, of course, but that took a few minutes in addition to the time I was unconscious. And I didn't feel restricted by the lack of air. I wasn't even breathing. And I felt that I didn't need to!"

"That is peculiar," she said meditatively. "Tell me, do you know a man named Goat Hennessey?"

"You're the second person who's asked me that recently," said Dark. "I knew him well, many years ago, but I haven't seen him in years. Why do you ask?"

"Because the only case I've heard about of any human being able to live without oxygen in the Martian atmosphere involved some genetic experiments of Goat Hennessey, before the government made him stop them and destroy the creatures he'd been experimenting with."

Dark laughed.

"I can assure you I'm not one of Goat's genetic experiments," he said. "Goat and I were colleagues in this rebel movement twenty-five years ago, before I was hit by a period of amnesia that I've just come out of."

She stared at him.

"A twenty-five year period of amnesia? Impossible! You're not more than twenty-five years old," she said positively.

"If what people tell me is correct, I'm nearer sixty," said Dark. "Terrestrial years, of course."

"Of course. But I don't believe it."

Dark shrugged, and cut another bite of steak. He seemed to be enjoying his meal quite as much as though he were not her prisoner and she his captor—as, indeed, she was, too.

They chatted pleasantly throughout the meal and Maya found, somewhat to her surprise, that she was talking about herself a great deal to this pale-eyed man. She told him of her childhood on Mars, among the Martians, and of going to Earth to live with her uncle, a World Senator who had had close and profitable connections with Marscorp.

She went on to tell of her decision to become an agent of the terrestrial government, despite her uncle's objections but as a result of his often-expressed enthusiasm for the government's role in developing the planetary colonies; and of her assignment to Mars to ferret out a rebel headquarters which had eluded the best efforts of the Martian government. She even told him how she had met Nuwell and fallen in love with him.

Some time after the meal's conclusion, she suddenly stopped in mid-sentence.

"What's the matter?" asked Dark.

"I just realized that you're my prisoner," she answered, smiling at him. "Frankly, I'm not sure what to do with you. We can't just sit here in the dining room all night."

"Why not go out and sit on the terrace?" he suggested. "They say that Solis Lacus is a beautiful sight when Phobos is up and moving."

"And a shadowed terrace is a very convenient place from which to attempt an escape," she countered.

"Look," he said, "there's no point in making the evening more difficult than it is. I very definitely intend to get away from you and get out of here during the next two days if I can, but I'm enjoying this conversation. If I promise that I won't attempt an escape in the next two hours, are you willing to go up on the terrace for a while?"

She studied his face carefully. It was a handsome, earnest face, full of strength, full of wisdom, with a touch of weariness.

"All right," she said at last. "But I warn you that if my trust is misplaced and you do attempt to escape, I'll burn you down without compunction."

They went up together, quite as casually as might any two guests relaxing at the resort, and found chairs in the semi-darkness overlooking the moonlit lowland.

Deimos hung near the zenith, a tiny globe of light, virtually stationary. Phobos, larger and brighter, was not long risen, and it moved swiftly and smoothly across the sky, like the cold searchlight of some giant aircraft. Touched and transformed by the shifting shadows, Maya and Dark sat and chatted like old friends.

Dark talked now, and he told her of his past life, of his coming to Mars, of his joining the rebel movement upon realizing how the government was holding back man's progress toward Martian self-sufficiency. He spoke soberly, with intense conviction, and Maya, listening, began to realize that there was another side to this conflict than the one she had been taught.

She began to waver and to wonder, for the grave voice of this man was like a deep music she had never heard before but seemed to remember from some time before there was hearing, a music that touched the depths of her being.

Then his arm slid around her waist and he drew her gently toward him. For an instant, she responded, turning her face upward.

And, on that instant, she remembered.

With a lightning twist, she was free, and on her feet before him. She stepped back, and the lighter-gun was in her hand.

"I thought you said I could trust you," she said coldly. "Evidently, I was foolish to do so."

He looked up at her, and there was nothing but surprise on his face. Then, slowly, he smiled at her.

"It depends on your interpretation of the word," he said. "I was merely attempting to kiss you, my dear."

She let her hand sag, feeling rather foolish.

"Well, don't," she said, her sharpness covering her confusion. "We aren't lovers, Mr. Kensington."

"No," he said, quite seriously. "And I find that I rather regret that we aren't."

She stood looking at him, fighting off a sneaking regret of her own that he hadn't succeeded in his intention.

"I think this moonlight has had an unfortunate effect on us both," she said. "We'd better go inside. Besides, if I'm to keep watch over you all night, I want to get into something more practical than an evening gown."

Without protest, Dark preceded her inside. They went to the manager's office, and Maya issued instructions to Gren.

"Have a maid move my things from my third-floor room to a room on the top floor," she ordered. "We'll wait here until it's done."

When the maid brought Maya the key to the new room, she and Dark took the elevator to it. As soon as they were inside, she locked the door behind them.

"I'm going into the bathroom to change clothes," she said precisely. "The window to this room is six floors above a stone courtyard and I don't think you can jump that far without being killed, even on Mars. Since these windows don't open, I'll hear you if you break it to get out, and I can burn you long before you can climb down the face of the wall."

The lighter-gun in her hand, she went into the bathroom and closed the door behind her.

She had just stripped off the evening gown when she heard the bathroom door lock from the outside. A moment later, there was the crashing sound of breaking glass.

Calmly, Maya burned off the lock of the bathroom door with the little heatgun. She pushed it open and went out into the room in her underwear. Dark was in the process of gingerly climbing through the broken window.

"It's a long fall, Dark," she said.

He looked back over his shoulder. He smiled ruefully, and came back into the room.

"Well, it was worth a try," he said philosophically.

He surveyed her with frankly admiring eyes and added:

"And it was worth failing, for the view."

She turned pink. But, without taking her eyes off him, she reached back into the bathroom, got the tunic and trousers she had laid out, and slipped them on.

"I think it would be better if we go down and sit in the middle of the lobby," she said, unlocking the door to the room. "That way, you'll have farther to run if you try to get away."

They went down and found comfortable seats. They sat there, talking, to all casual appearance two of the chateau's guests. Gradually, the conversation moved back to its earlier informal and friendly terms.

How long they sat chatting, Maya did not know, for she was wrapped up in her enjoyment of the things Dark said and his attitude toward life. But after a time she realized that no more guests were sitting in the lobby or moving through it. They were the only ones there, except for Gren, sitting morosely behind the registration desk.

"Just how do you propose to get any sleep and watch me at the same time?" asked Dark.

"I don't," she answered, smiling. "If you can stay awake for two nights, so can I."

"You forget, young lady," he retorted. "I don't have to."

With that, he stretched out unceremoniously on the sofa on which he had been sitting, clasped his hands behind his head and closed his eyes. Within a very short time, he was obviously and genuinely sound asleep.

Maya sat and watched him, piqued and a little nonplussed. She could hardly afford to go to sleep, too. Her only course was to stay awake, to sit there and watch him sleeping comfortably and soundly. It was not a pleasant prospect, for two nights.

She sat, heavy-eyed, and racked her brain for some solution, and silently cursed Gren for refusing to give her the help she needed. Dark slept on, and a faint smile touched his lips. Then Maya found herself thinking pleasantly over the things they had talked about during the long evening, and admiring this man and liking him....

She woke up.

With a start, she woke up, realizing that she had been asleep. She was not sitting in the chair any more, but curled up comfortably on a sofa, her head pillowed like a child's against–against what?

Against Dark's chest! He was awake, sitting up, smiling down at her, and she was cradled in the curve of his arm. And the little lighter-gun was no longer in her hand.

She did not react violently to the sudden realization. She sighed, almost happily, and murmured to him:

"So you win, after all. I think I'm glad, Dark. Now you can go, if you want to."

He shook his head.

"I'm glad you feel that way about it, Maya, but I'm afraid it's too late. I really shouldn't have stayed around to serve as your pillow till you awoke."

There was something in his face that caused her to sit up suddenly.

Two uniformed men stood there in the lobby before them, relaxed but watchful, regulation heatguns dangling from their hands. As she sat up, one of them touched his cap and spoke to her:

"We're police officers from Ophir, Miss Cara Nome. Mr. Eli called from Mars City and directed us to drive over here and help you guard the prisoner until his arrival."

She rose angrily.

"I didn't ask for your help, so you may go," she said, aware of Dark's surprised gaze on her. "I made a mistake in identification."

The policeman who had spoken shook his head.

"I'm sorry," he said. "We're acting on Mr. Eli's orders, not yours. We'll have to hold Mr. Kensington until Mr. Eli arrives."

She glared at them. The one who had spoken was big and burly and efficient-looking. The other was sallow and silent, with a deadly cast to his thin face.

Then she saw her lighter-gun, lying on the lobby floor beside the chair in which she had gone to sleep.

She bent down, casually, and picked it up. She straightened, the little instrument ready in her hand.

"This is not a cigaret lighter, but a heatgun," she said flatly. "I'm in charge here, and I say Mr. Kensington is to be permitted to go free. If any effort is made to stop him, I'll burn you down."

Both police heatguns swung up in short arcs and trained on her. The burly policeman spoke gently.

"I'm sorry, Miss Cara Nome, but we're under orders from Mr. Eli, and we intend to follow them," he said. "I'd hate to see you injured, but if you blast either of us the other one will burn off your hand."

"No, Maya!" exclaimed Dark, getting to his feet. "Don't! There's no point in your getting hurt for my sake."

She ignored him.

"Drop those heatguns, both of you, or I blast!" she snapped, almost hysterically.

Then Dark hurled himself bodily at the two men.

The thin-faced man swung his heatgun around to meet Dark's charge. Maya twisted the lighter-gun toward him, and at the same moment the burly policeman threw himself against her. Her heat beam singed the thin-faced one's shoulder, then she collapsed under the impact of the other's body.

As she fell, she saw the almost invisible beam of the thin-faced policeman's heatgun strike Dark directly in the stomach, burning away the cloth, burning a great gaping hole in his abdomen. Dark slid to the floor, writhing, gasping, clutching his stomach.

Her lighter-gun knocked from her hand, Maya struggled, half-dazed, to her feet. The burly policeman had swung his own gun on the prostrate Dark, but the other one, grimacing with the pain of his wounded shoulder, stopped him.

"Let him be," he said. "I like to watch them die."

With a wail, Maya dropped to Dark's side. She cradled his head against her breast and sobbed as he died in her arms.

9

From the time she saw Dark Kensington die until Nuwell's arrival at the Chateau Nectaris a day later, Maya remained in her room, half in shock, half in an agony of sorrow and remorse.

She was so exhausted by her ordeal that she did sleep, but it was fitfully and without genuine rest. She had her meals sent up to her room, and ate automatically, not tasting the food.

Rationally, she could in no way blame herself for Dark's death, but that did not prevent her feeling strongly that her insistence on tracking down the fugitives from the Childress Barber College had made her, directly, his slayer. Her feeling of distress was much deeper and more personal than normal regret at having brought about the death of a friendly enemy while in pursuit of her duty.

Maya realized that in those few hours she had been with Dark and talked to him, something had taken root and flowered that had changed her whole outlook on existence. She did not want to call it love; she was a very practical young woman and did not believe in love on such short notice. But, in examining her feelings, she was at a loss as to what else to call it.

She had felt a powerful attraction to this man, a tremendous admiration and liking for him, a feeling of *belonging* in his presence. She had sensed his strength. It had appalled her when she had had to oppose herself to him in keeping him captive, but in other circumstances she felt it was the sort of strength she could depend on. Willingly, she thought now, she, could have dispensed with everything else in her life, and followed Dark

Kensington wherever he chose to wander, a fugitive, among the deserts and lowlands.

And Nuwell? Her feeling for him had not changed. She was still attracted to him and she still admired him. But the admiration she had felt for his sharp, sardonic handling of his opponents in a court of law seemed a little shallow and a little immature in comparison to the sudden onrush of what she sensed about Dark.

Since her early teens, she had been an eager enemy of those rebels whom she conceived to be disrupting the orderly settlement of Mars, and her desire to contribute to the defeat of those rebels had been a disciplining, integrating force in her personality. Yet, in only a few short hours of quiet talk, Dark had cut the foundation from that force and dissipated it.

If only she had not delayed, if only she had made up her mind decisively to what she felt now ... Dark need not have died, she could have freed him, and together they could have left Solis Lacus. With him, she would have fought as hard for the rebel cause as, in the past, she had fought against it.

But now it was too late. And, moping tearfully in her room, she found that she didn't care any more, one way or another, about the struggle between Marscorp and the rebels.

By the time Nuwell arrived from Mars City, she had regained control over her feelings. When he telephoned her in her room, she went down to the lobby to meet him, pale but composed.

She had a strange feeling as she came out into the big lobby, arching up above its balconies, a feeling as though she had been away in a distant land for a very long time and was just returning to the world she had known all her life. In this returning, she looked upon things with new ideas, and they did not appear the same as before.

This was the same spacious lobby across which she had walked to register when she came to Solis Lacus from Mars City a few days ago. It was the same lobby in which, looking down from the balcony, she had seen Dark Kensington arriving. It was the same lobby in which she had sat with Dark and talked for so long. But it seemed a strange place, a different place, one that looked like the lobby she remembered but in which she had never walked before.

Nuwell was standing across the lobby with the two police officers from Ophir, beside a long wooden box that rested on the floor next to the registration counter. Behind the counter, Quelman Gren, the manager of Chateau Nectaris, was sorting the day's mail.

Nuwell saw her, detached himself from the others and came across the lobby to meet her. As he approached, she experienced the same feeling toward him that she had felt toward the lobby: he was like someone she had known, but a different person.

There was a worried frown on Nuwell's face, and he managed to get something of disapproval in his greeting kiss.

"It's lucky I called Ophir and had those men sent over here," were his first words. "If they hadn't gotten here when they did, that rebel might have killed you and escaped. I told you, Maya, not to try to handle a situation like that."

"It was very astute of you to send them over," answered Maya dryly. "I should have thought of it myself."

"That's exactly why you shouldn't try to handle such things alone," said Nuwell, apparently somewhat mollified.

Maya looked into his face, a handsome, youthful face bearing a slightly peeved expression, and she thought two things: she thought of the long and intensive training she had undergone as a terrestrial agent, and she contemplated just how effectively Nuwell might have handled Dark's capture, had Nuwell been in her place.

"Come on, Maya, let's clear this up, so we can get out of here and get back to Mars City," said Nuwell, and led her across the lobby to the two policemen and the wooden box.

The two men from Ophir greeted her with a certain embarrassment, and seemed relieved when she smiled wanly at them.

"These men have told me how the rebel had turned the tables and gained the advantage of you before their arrival," said Nuwell. "They say that before he was killed, he confessed to them that he was Dark Kensington, one of the major rebel leaders who escaped from the Childress Barber College. I believe that coincides with your identification of him, doesn't it?"

"Yes," answered Maya in a low voice. "He was Dark Kensington. I saw him once at the college, and he identified himself to me then as a supervisor."

She did not feel called on to say anything more, and to tell Nuwell what Dark himself had told her about the rebellion and his part in it.

"Very good," said Nuwell with satisfaction. "We've captured the Chief, the peculiar-looking individual who escaped by driving his copter through the city dome. All the indications are that he and Kensington were the two top figures in the rebellion. I think all that's needed now is for you to identify the body positively as Kensington, Maya."

He indicated the wooden box, which lay, lidless, on the floor. Reluctantly, Maya stepped up to it, and looked down into it.

The pain which distorted Dark's face when he lay writhing from the heatgun blast was gone from his features. They were calm and peaceful in death.

Maya gazed down at his face wistfully, sorrowfully, then turned away.

"Well?" asked Nuwell impatiently.

"Yes," she murmured. "That's Dark Kensington."

"Very good," said Nuwell, and turned to the two men. "We'll take the body to the hydroponic farm for the vats," he said. "There'll be others after the trials and executions of the rebels we've captured."

"Do you have to do that?" protested Maya. "Why can't you give the man a decent burial out here in the lowland?"

"Don't interfere in matters which are none of your affair," replied Nuwell brusquely. "Bodies of criminals are always sent to the vats. They're constantly short of bodies, as it is, and we can't very well send them corpses of law-abiding citizens."

He turned away. As Maya accompanied him across the corridor, the two men from Ophir began nailing the lid on the wooden box that contained Dark Kensington's remains.

At the elevator, Nuwell said:

"Get your things packed as soon as you can. I want to go back to Mars City right away by copter. I have some things I want to talk to you about, very seriously, but they can wait until we're airborne."

"Why by copter?" asked Maya. "Groundcar is faster."

For the first time, Nuwell's face broke into a genuine smile, and his ordinary charming self shone through.

"Because," he replied drolly, "I've just made that trip by groundcar, and every bone in my body aches. It may be slower, but I want to go back by air, where there aren't as many bumps!"

Maya was able to laugh at this. She went up to her room.

It did not take her long to pack, and to dress in a tunic and trousers for travel. When she came back down to the lobby, Nuwell was waiting, and they took a groundcar from the chateau to the dome airlock.

The three government agents who had come with Nuwell from Mars City had the helicopter ready for them on the flat lowland just beyond the airlock. As the groundcar emerged onto the sage-covered plain, the men were helping the two policemen from Ophir unload the box containing Dark Kensington's remains from another groundcar and load it into the baggage bay of the copter. Nuwell and Maya slipped into their marsuits, secured the helmets and climbed out of the groundcar. Nuwell gave his men some final instructions to follow before returning to Mars City by groundcar. Then he and Maya went aboard the copter.

They strapped themselves in the seats. Nuwell sealed the copter door, and released oxygen from the tanks into the interior. When the dials showed the air to be breathable, he and Maya removed their helmets, Nuwell started the motor and the craft lifted slowly and smoothly into the air above the Solis Lacus Lowland.

Nuwell headed the copter northwestward. As soon as they were well on course, he turned to Maya with a stern expression on his face.

"There's one thing I can't understand at all," he said severely. "What madness possessed you to resist those men I sent over from Ophir, and attempt to help Kensington escape?"

She looked at him steadily without replying.

What should she answer? Could she say, "I discovered that I had fallen in love with Dark Kensington. I found that his reasons for the rebellion made sense to me, and that you and the government and Marscorp are wrong"?

What would Nuwell's reaction be if she told this truth?

But it could do no good to say that. It could do the rebels no good, because now they were scattered and defeated. It could do Dark no good, because he was dead. She did not think she would suffer personally from such a revelation, but it could only hurt Nuwell, who loved her.

So, at last, she said:

"Nuwell, I'd rather not talk about that. I didn't succeed, so can we forget it?"

"I think it's best that we do," agreed Nuwell. "The only thing I can think is that you were slightly hysterical over Kensington's having gained the upper hand, after the strain of guarding him for so long, and your action was an unconscious expression of resentment at their having to take over his custody where you had failed. But we might have learned a great deal through questioning the man at length, and that action of yours made it necessary for them to kill him."

Nuwell could not know how deeply those words struck her. She turned her face away from him, and the tears came to her eyes.

"At any rate," went on Nuwell, unaware, "I think this demonstrates that these espionage activities have been far too much of a strain for you, and I think it's time you stopped. We have one of the two major leaders captured and the other one dead, and I don't think they're going to give us much more trouble even if we don't locate all the fugitives. So I want you to give up this idea of wandering around from city to city, helping identify rebels."

"I think you're right," she agreed in a choked voice. She had no more interest now, certainly, in tracking down rebels.

"And," continued Nuwell, even more firmly, "marry me when we get back to Mars City."

Well, why not? Nuwell loved her. What else was there for her?

"Yes, I'll do that, too," she said. "As soon as we get back, I'll make out my report, and send my resignation with it back on the first ship to Earth. Then I'll marry you, Nuwell."

His face was radiant and triumphant as he turned to her. He put his arm around her shoulders, drew her to him and kissed her.

The helicopter flew northwestward. Passing over the Solis Lacus Lowland, it crossed the Thaumasia Desert and the Tithonius Lacus Lowland, and whirred above the

Desert of Candor. Ahead of it, after a time, there rose on the horizon the white stone forms of a distant group of buildings.

Nuwell dropped the helicopter lower. He angled it down, and in a short time landed it on the desert near one of the four buildings of the Canfell Hydroponic Farm.

As he and Maya donned their marshelmets, a group of marsuited men emerged from the building's airlock and came across the sand toward them.

Maya stared curiously out the copter window. She had heard of this government experimental station, but had not visited it before.

"This is another reason I wanted to take a copter," explained Nuwell, releasing the air from the copter's interior. "There aren't any roads to this place, and I didn't want to drive a groundcar across the desert to bring Kensington's body here."

They emerged from the copter as the group from the building approached. Nuwell greeted the five of them and introduced them to Maya. Four of them were strangers to her, but the fifth she remembered: Goat Hennessey, white-bearded and watery-eyed.

"How are you adjusting to your new work here, Dr. Hennessey?" Nuwell asked him.

"Very well," answered Goat in his cracked voice. "They're using a different approach from mine, but I find it extremely interesting."

Remembering Goat's earlier experiments at Ultra Vires, it occurred to Maya to be grateful that Dark had not fallen alive into the hands of these people at the Canfell Hydroponic Farm.

Their entire stop lasted only a few minutes. Nuwell refused an invitation to remain overnight, explaining that he was anxious to get on to Mars City. The others unloaded Dark's coffin and moved with it back toward the building. Nuwell and Maya climbed back into the copter, and shortly they were airborne again and the buildings of the Canfell Hydroponic Farm were receding behind and below them.

Nuwell guided the copter almost straight westward now. It passed over Candor and buzzed out over the broad Xanthe Desert.

And here trouble developed. Without warning, the engine coughed and stopped. Nuwell worked frantically at the controls, to no avail. As the big blades slowed in their rotation, the copter sank, slowly at first, then ever more swiftly, to the surface of the desert. They donned marshelmets hurriedly.

It struck with a terrific crash, which would have hurled them through the windows had they not been strapped down. The entire body of the copter crumpled in on itself, and it came to rest, a collapsed wreck, with the two of them sitting in its midst, miraculously uninjured.

There was no question of trying to start the engines or fly the machine. It was a total wreck. Nuwell tried the radio without success.

"What in space went wrong with the thing?" he demanded angrily. "I know it wasn't short of fuel. There's nothing left for us to do but walk, I'm afraid, Maya."

"Back to the hydroponic farm?"

"No, we've come too far. By my chart, we're not far from Ultra Vires. I think we'd better try to make it for the night, and if Goat left his radio equipment in working order we'll call for help. If not, the only thing I know to do is to head for Ophir."

Ultra Vires—Maya remembered it with a shudder. The grim, black bastion in the desert where Goat Hennessey had worked with grotesque, twisted caricatures of humans.

They fumbled about the wreck to find the minimum emergency supplies they thought they would need, and started westward on foot.

10

Happy Thurbelow finished sweeping the long barracks and leaned wearily on his broom. That is, he didn't lean on it, or it would have collapsed him to the floor, but he made the gesture. Why, he wondered, didn't the Masters make the Toughs sweep their own barracks? Perhaps the Toughs couldn't be made, or perhaps the Masters did it just from an excess of cruelty.

Happy's monstrously bloated body sagged, and his skin felt dangerously dry and tight. Happy was so adipose that his hands engulfed the broom handle like a toothpick; under the transparent skin, his flesh was clear and translucent, and there could be seen the tiny red lines of the branching veins. Happy was like a jellyfish, in huge human form.

"Shadow!" he called in a high, grating voice. "I'm going below."

Shadow appeared disconcertingly, ten feet away. Dark-skinned Shadow looked at him silently with white-rimmed eyes. Then Shadow turned and disappeared, as only Shadow could.

Hanging up the broom, Happy waddled to the iron-barred gate that prevented entrance to a downward-plunging ramp. He pressed a button beside it and waited.

He looked out the window beside the gate. The sands of the Desert of Candor stretched orange and bleak under the bronze sky. Somewhere out there to the south, across those sands, under that sky, lay the shining dome of Ophir.

The window would be easily broken, and it was large enough for even Happy's bulky body to pass through. But the oxygen-scant air of Mars would sear his lungs to quick death without a helmet; and even if it would not, Happy's skin would dry and crack in a few hours of that outside air, and he would die in slower agony.

"What is the purpose of your call?" asked an impersonal voice from the loudspeaker beside the barred gate.

"I have finished my task, Master," said Happy, puffing a little. "I seek your grace to go below."

The loudspeaker said no more, but after a moment the gate stirred and lifted into the ceiling. Happy went through it gratefully, and waddled down the gently sloping ramp. The gate descended behind him.

Happy did not know whether Shadow had come through the open gate with him, but it didn't matter. Shadow could slip easily through the bars when he wished.

At the foot of the ramp was a vast, low cavern, stretching out of sight in all directions. It was dim, shading into the darkness of distance. Its floor was water, flat water, subdivided into large rectangular vats. In most of the vats vegetation grew in various stages, greening under the ultraviolet rays that radiated from the low roof. Between the vats ran straight, narrow walkways of packed earth.

Happy waddled along one of the walkways until he found an empty vat. He lowered himself over its edge and sank happily into the still, cool water, like a hippopotamus submerging. He immersed himself completely, then lay back in the water, with only his face floating barely above the surface.

Shadow appeared, apparently out of nowhere, and sat down on the edge of the vat, letting his flat legs dangle into the water.

"Nothing like it," proclaimed Happy, splashing a little. "Nothing on Mars like it. You ought to come on in, Shadow. As flat as you are, you ought to float on the surface without any trouble at all."

Shadow nodded silently, but made no move.

"I don't see why the Toughs can't take care of their own barracks," complained Happy, returning to the subject closest to his displeasure. "You reckon the Toughs are actually the rebels, and the Masters can't make them do anything?"

Shadow shook his head, but whether in negation or disclaimer of knowledge, Happy could not interpret.

Happy flinched, and shifted in the vat.

"There's still part of a skeleton in here," he announced. "I thought this was an empty one."

Moving, he flinched again. With purpose, he aroused himself and ploughed to the edge of the vat.

"I've got to find another vat," he said. "I can't take a nap if I'm going to get punched in the fanny with bones every five minutes."

He heaved himself over the edge onto the walkway with difficulty, and got slowly to his feet. Shadow lifted his feet out of the vat, stood up and vanished.

Happy knew how Shadow was able to disappear so suddenly, and it did not disturb him. Seen directly from front or rear, Shadow had the dimensions of a normal, black-skinned man. But Shadow was flat, no thicker than half an inch. When Shadow turned sidewise, he vanished to the sight.

Occasionally, Happy wondered how Shadow happened to be, and why he was here in the caverns, but it was not the sort of thing to bother his mind for very long.

Happy moved along the walkways, peering into the vats which appeared to be empty. He assumed Shadow was following him; Shadow always did.

Around corners, he came upon blubbery creatures like himself, tending the plants. They nodded greeting at him, and Happy nodded back.

His search was discouraging. All the vats not filled with plants seemed to have corpses in them, in varying stages of decomposition.

Around one corner, Happy came upon a Tough, lounging in the walkway. The Tough was a compact, muscular youth, with bullet head, sullen eyes and hard mouth. He looked as though he lounged with hands in pockets, but, like Happy and all the others, he was naked, so that was just an impression.

Happy stopped. He and his soft kind avoided the Toughs when they could. The Tough looked at him with disinterested eyes, then looked away.

Happy was uncertain what to do or say. His impulse was to turn and go back, but he did not quite dare.

"Are you a rebel, Tough?" he burbled the first thing in his mind, for lack of something else to say.

The Tough looked at him contemptuously. Then, suddenly, the Tough's hard eyes flared with savage excitement and he moved swiftly on Happy. As he began to turn in panic, Happy saw from the corner of his eye another Tough racing around the corner of the walkway to come upon him from behind.

The Tough in front of him reached him and began pummeling him viciously with his fists, the hard fists sinking like painful hammers deep into Happy's flesh with every blow. Happy bleated in fright and distress, trying ineffectually to ward off his attacker.

Then, out of nowhere, Shadow flashed in like a lightning bolt on the other Tough as he had almost reached Happy. There was a brief, squalling tangle and the Tough pitched headlong into a plant-choked vat.

Shadow vanished and reappeared, intermittently, like a flashing light. The first Tough, seeing what had happened to his cohort, ceased pummeling Happy abruptly and took to his heels. He vanished around a corner.

The vanquished Tough climbed out of the vat, sputtering and cursing, and fled in the other direction.

"Oh, my! Oh, my!" exclaimed Happy to the now-invisible Shadow. "What wicked creatures!"

Sore and shaken, he moved on down the walkway, his search now intensified by the need for wetness to soothe his injured flesh.

He came upon a vat without vegetation and, at first joyous glance, thought it empty. Then, disappointment, a comparatively fresh body floated in it, just under the surface. It was the body of a man. Naked, it was smooth and plump with the water that had seeped into its tissues, and it was a uniform dead-white all over, like the belly of a fish. The face and lips were monochrome white, the hair was bleached, and when it opened its eyes, they were so colorless that the action was almost unnoticeable.

Realizing, Happy was paralyzed with shock.

The dead creature's eyes moved from side to side, then stopped, fixing on Happy. Its chest began to rise and fall slowly, with breathing—*under water.*

"Shadow!" squeaked Happy helplessly.

Shadow appeared beside him.

"Shadow, it's alive," whispered Happy, desperately frightened.

The two stood side by side, staring breathlessly down into the water. The creature in the vat moved its hands tentatively, it opened its mouth and closed it. Then it stirred with purpose, turned and climbed up over the side of the vat, dripping like a weird creature from the depths of the sea.

It stood up before them, dripping.

The man bent slightly and belched forth a great quantity of water from his lungs. He straightened, and breathed in the air in great, satisfied gasps.

"I'm Dark Kensington," he said in a rusty voice. "Where is this?"

At his words, Shadow disappeared.

Dark Kensington. Had Maya seen him now, she could not possibly have recognized him. The muscular body and dark, handsome face were bloated and pale. The black hair was bleached to pale seaweed, and the blue eyes were completely colorless now.

"This is the Canfell Hydroponic Farm," answered Happy, gaining a little courage. "Under the surface of the Desert of Candor."

"The Desert of Candor?" repeated Dark, and the pale lips twisted in a smile. "They hauled me quite a way. I was at Solis Lacus."

"How did you get here?" asked Happy with sudden eagerness. "Only dead people are thrown in the vats, to make chemicals for the plants. How could you stay alive under water?"

"I imagine I can breathe water for the same reason I can still live after a heat beam burned my guts out, but I don't know what that reason is. I imagine that the first step in finding out is to get out of this place."

"You can't get away from here," said Happy positively. "Nobody ever has."

"We'll see," said Dark confidently. "I gather you and your companion are some sort of prisoners."

"Slaves," corrected Happy with unaccustomed bitterness. "The Jellies are slaves, to work in the vats. I don't know if the Toughs are slaves, too, but the Masters let them sleep in barracks on the surface. Shadow's not either a Jelly or a Tough, and I don't know if he's a slave. Shadow's just Shadow."

"Before you go on," interrupted Dark, "I seem to be extraordinarily hungry."

Happy twittered and quivered. He moved hurriedly around a corner to one of the storage vats, and returned in a moment with a supply of the tasteless gelatin that was their food here. Dark fell to greedily, and Happy, his tongue loosed by this new companionship, started feeding him information in a steady stream.

"I don't know how they get us here," said Happy. "We aren't born here, but something happens to our memories. We can't stay up in the dry air very long, or our skin cracks and our flesh collapses. You see, our tissues are mostly water.

"Everybody down here's like me. Everybody but the Toughs. You'll see them. I don't know how they got here, either, or what use they are. They don't work like we do.

"And Shadow. He's different. Shadow likes me. He stays with me all the time. And then there's Old Beard. He hides down here, and I don't think the Masters know he's here. He's very old and very wise."

"Who are the Masters?" asked Dark curiously, between mouthfuls. "And what sort of work do you do for them?"

"They're the people who run the hydroponic farm. They're normal men, like you—I mean, like you would be if you weren't swollen up and pale like the bodies that are thrown in the vats.

"Old Beard knows; he's very wise. He calls the Masters 'Marscorp.' I don't know why, but it seems that before I lost my memory I knew a language where *corp* meant *body*. Like *corpse*, you know. Maybe it has something to do with the bodies they put in the vats.

"Old Beard says that the Masters are developing Martian foods that we can eat without dying, and he must be right, because sometimes they bring down some hard foods and make some of us eat them instead of gelatin. But those who eat the hard foods always die, so I don't suppose they've succeeded yet, except some of the Toughs. Some of the Toughs have eaten the hard food without dying, sometimes, but they got pretty sick. And then—"

"Hold on! Wait a minute!" exclaimed Dark, holding up a restraining hand. "I know what Marscorp is, and I'm not surprised they're behind it. But I'm trying to digest all this you're throwing at me."

Happy fell silent, reluctantly, and Dark cogitated deeply.

Happy fidgeted, anxious to speak but afraid to interrupt Dark's thoughts.

And then Shadow reappeared. Shadow appeared out of nowhere, and made gestures at Happy. Happy glanced at Dark, timidly. At last, he gained courage to speak.

"Shadow tells me–" he began, then cringed when Dark looked up in surprise. Dark gestured to him to go on.

"Shadow tells me," said Happy, "that Old Beard wants to see you. Will you go with us to Old Beard?"

"Certainly," agreed Dark. "From what you tell me, I'm rather anxious to meet Old Beard, too."

He followed Happy and the alternately visible and invisible Shadow along the paths that twisted among the vats for some distance. At last they ducked into some luxuriant foliage that hung over to form a bower above the space between two vats.

Old Beard sat there, in a corner of the dimness, pale eyes fixed silently on the trio. Old Beard was not so very old. He appeared to be in robust middle age, although his skin was very pale from long existence underground. His hair and heavy beard were long and untrimmed, and were a deep iron-gray.

"Thank you for coming," said Old Beard in a deep, resonant voice that bespoke strength and bore an undertone of bitter determination. "It is safer for me not to move around too much in the open except at certain hours."

"I was glad to come, because I'm sure you can help me and I may be able to help you, too," said Dark. "I'm Dark Kensington."

"So Shadow told me. I find this extremely interesting."

"You've heard of me, then?" asked Dark.

Old Beard laughed, deeply.

"More interesting than that," he said. "Once, before I was marooned here and Happy's people came to know me as Old Beard, I had a name of my own."

He stroked his beard, and favored Dark with a shrewd look from his pale eyes.

"Yes," said Old Beard, "I've heard of Dark Kensington, and there never was but one Dark Kensington, as far as I knew. That's why I find it so interesting. You see, I'm Dark Kensington!"

11

The Xanthe Desert stretched red and barren on all sides of the plodding couple, the sands unbroken by the form of plant or stone or any living thing, all the way to the tight horizon of Mars. Above them, the small, glittering sun slid down the copper-hued sky slowly toward the west.

It was remarkable, thought Maya, how smooth and flat the desert looked from the air, and how rough and rolling it was when one had to walk across the packed sand. They had been walking for hours and, despite the gentle gravity of Mars, she was getting very tired.

"It's farther than I thought," said Nuwell, his voice distorted by the marshelmet speaker. "Distances on the chart are deceptive. We may not reach Ultra Vires by night."

Maya did not answer. Again, as she had many weeks before, she was in the grip of a sensation that this desert through which they walked was only a surface thing, a shimmering mask to the reality which lay behind it. That reality seemed very deep, very significant, and she felt that she was on the verge of comprehending it, but could not quite grasp it.

She was a little irritated at Nuwell for speaking when he did. If his voice had not interrupted her probing emotions, she felt, she might have broken through to that reality she sensed.

"Nuwell," she said, giving it up, "I'm going to have to rest a while. If we don't make it by night, we don't make it. There's always tomorrow, and I'm tired."

Reluctantly, he consented, and they sat down together on the sand. Nuwell pulled a chart out of his marsuit pocket and began to study it. Maya lay back, clasped her hands behind her helmet and closed her eyes, gratefully feeling the tired muscles relax and the perspiration that bathed her begin to dissolve in the gentle circulation of the marsuit's temperature-control system.

"Maya!" exclaimed Nuwell suddenly. "Look! We're going to be rescued!"

She sat up and looked in the direction of his pointing finger. On the horizon to the northeast was a cloud of dust, too placid and stationary to be a sandstorm.

They stood up, and Nuwell spoke hastily into his helmet radio on the conventional emergency band.

"Attention, groundcar! Attention, groundcar! We're afoot and in trouble. We're afoot, due southwest from your position. Help, please. Attention, groundcar!"

There was no radio reply in the ensuing silence. But all at once it was as though a deep and alien voice spoke within the depths of Maya's mind:

"We see you."

Startled, she looked curiously at Nuwell. But he evidently had not had the same experience. He was chattering into the radio frantically again.

"They're evidently not tuned in on the emergency band, Nuwell," she said to him. "But they're coming almost directly toward us. They're bound to see us soon, if they haven't already."

"That's true," said Nuwell, and added sourly: "But they ought to be tuned in. It's required by law."

The dustcloud moved closer slowly, too slowly for a groundcar. They were able to discern a dark nucleus below and in front of it. Then Nuwell said:

"In the name of space! It isn't a groundcar, Maya. It's a band of Martians! Let's get out of here!"

He started to walk on swiftly, but Maya stood her ground.

"Don't be silly," she said. "Martians won't hurt us. I was raised among them."

Nuwell stopped and returned reluctantly to her side.

"They may not hurt us, but why wait for them?" he demanded, and there was a touch of hysterical fright to his tone. "Let's go on, Maya!"

"We may very well have gotten off course in trying to go straight to Ultra Vires," replied Maya logically. "That may be why we've not sighted it yet. The Martians will know where it is, and meeting them may prevent us from getting lost in the desert."

Nuwell subsided, but she could see from the expression on his face that he was in a blue funk. This puzzled her. She could not understand why anyone would be afraid of Martians. They were huge, and ugly, and alien, but they were not inimical to humans.

When the Martians came near enough, Maya waved her arms at them and started off to meet them, Nuwell following her at a little distance. The Martians changed course slightly and came toward them.

Maya called childhood memories to her aid. She turned her helmet speaker to its maximum volume, and spoke to them in their own language, in the deepest tones possible to her.

"Children of the past, we seek that place in the desert which is called 'Ultra Vires' by humans," she said. "Can you show us the direction in which we must travel?"

The Martians gathered around her, towering over her. There were four of them. Their huge chests moved slowly, mixing oxygen from their great humps with the surrounding air. Their thin arms hung limp at their sides, and their big ears were pricked forward toward her. Their huge, dark eyes seemed to look through her and beyond her.

"The sun moves toward this place, but there are no humans there now," boomed one of the Martians. "Nothing lives there now except small animals in the walls and corridors."

"This we know," answered Maya. "We wish to go there that we may communicate with other humans and have them come and get us."

She wanted to say that the supplies of oxygen in their marsuit tanks were inadequate to take them anywhere other than Ultra Vires, but she did not know how to say this properly in the Martian language.

But, to her astonishment, the Martian answered as though she had said it.

"If the breathing chemicals which you carry are at such a depleted stage, you cannot chance going astray," said the creature. "Rather than tell you the direction of this place, we shall accompany you there."

Throughout this conversation, Nuwell had been standing at Maya's side, his face bearing an expression of mingled curiosity, irritation and awe. Maya turned to him.

"The Martians say they will go with us to Ultra Vires, so we won't get lost," she told him.

"No!" he exclaimed vehemently. "Tell them we don't want them along. Tell them just to show us the way, and we'll go alone."

"Don't be ridiculous," replied Maya coldly, and indicated to the Martian that they were ready to accompany the group.

They moved off together toward the west, the four Martians and the two humans. Maya, feeling somewhat relieved that now they had expert help in reaching their goal, attempted to talk to Nuwell, but he refused to answer except in monosyllables. He was angry that she had agreed for the Martians to accompany them, and obviously was still very nervous at their presence.

So she talked instead with the Martian who had acted as spokesman for the group. Its name, she learned, was Qril.

"The place to which you go lies under an evil atmosphere," said Qril. "The human who abode there many years attempted to do things wrongly."

"We were there in the season before this one," answered Maya. "This was just before that human left."

"I already had read this in you," said Qril. "I also read in you that, as a child, you lived among us who are children of the past. Therefore, perhaps you knew before I spoke that an evil atmosphere remains at this place and has not yet been washed away by time."

"No, I was not taught such matters as a child," answered Maya. "But tell me, it is true that this man tried to do evil things, by human standards, but were Goat Hennessey's genetic experiments also evil by Martian standards?"

"You do not read what I have said quite correctly," replied Qril. "The evil atmosphere is left by the man, because what he did was evil by his own standards. I said only that he attempted to do things wrongly."

"What do you mean?" asked Maya.

"To explain to you, I must speak to you about things about which you already know partially," answered Qril. "Before you were born, the human you call Goat was one of a group of humans who sought ways to make humans independent of the spaceships which bring materials from Earth to Mars and create small islands of terrestrial conditions in the midst of the Martian environment. When they met the natural resistance of those humans who gain material advantage through operation of the spaceships, they came into the desert to be free to work.

"Seeking to get far from the men who resisted their work, this group of humans went to that area which you know as the Icaria Desert. Some of us who are children of the past live at that place sometimes, and these humans sought our help, knowing that we possess many remnants of the knowledge that our forefathers had.

"But we had difficulty helping them. They were attempting to follow two courses simultaneously, and both of them were wrong."

"I know something of those two courses," said Maya. "Some of them were trying to develop human extrasensory powers so that materials could be teleported from Earth, and the others were trying to change the human body physiologically so that humans could live under Martian conditions. But you say they were both wrong?"

"In each way that they followed, they sought to make humans partly like us, the children of the past," said Qril. "We have the power to communicate with our minds over a distance, and some of us are able to transport things with our minds over a distance. We do not need your rich terrestrial air, because we take oxygen directly from the soil and store it in our bodies for combustion purposes.

"But humans and the children of the past are different forms of life, and they cannot be made so much alike. It is possible for humans to develop mental powers similar to ours, but this course would leave them dependent upon importing materials from Earth, even though this would be by mind transmission instead of by spaceship. The other course they followed could not succeed, because the human body cannot be altered so that it is able to take oxygen from the soil and store it for later use."

"But you're wrong!" exclaimed Maya. "Goat Hennessey had succeeded in developing some humans who could live without oxygen in the air for a time. His experiments were imperfect, it's true, but they were able to do that."

"The imperfect humans that the human called Goat had developed were not what he thought," replied Qril. "We tried to help the humans to find the right course, but they could not understand us well. We tried to show them, by charts and example, that the proper way to adapt a human to Martian conditions was a different way.

"Because Earth is nearer the Sun, humans have a possibility that we do not have. What we tried to show

these humans was a method whereby they could change
the embryonic physiology so that the adult human would
be able to use the energy of solar radiations directly,
instead of depending on the energy of combustion of those
chemicals you call oxygen and carbon. This makes the
body independent of both air and food, and has the
advantage also of giving a far superior regenerative
power to the bodily tissues.

"The human, Goat, for reasons that are not known,
stole some of our charts and two of the pregnant female
humans, and continued his work at this place to which we
are going. But he thought he was still attempting to
change the physiology so that oxygen could be stored, and
therefore his experiments went wrongly."

"But he had your charts," objected Maya. "Even
though he was not making the alterations he thought he
was, how could he go wrong if he followed the charts?"

"The charts showed the changes to be made in the
embryonic cells, but they could not show the method
whereby the changes are made," replied Qril. "The
human, Goat, attempted to make these changes by
mechanical, surgical methods but these are too crude to
be successful. The method we utilize to make such
changes, which is the only right method, is to focus the
mental forces upon the embryo. I believe you would call it
psychokinesis."

Maya was vastly excited at this revelation.

"Then Goat's oldest experiments, the ones he called
Brute and Adam, were actually the ones on whom you
children of the past had performed the embryonic
changes!" she exclaimed. "They must have been the sons
of the pregnant women he kidnapped. That's why they
were more successful than the others!"

"That is true," said Qril. "We had completed the
change on only one of the two, therefore only that one
would develop into an adult who could live in complete
independence of air and food, if necessary. The other one

would never be able to do it for more than a short period without returning to terrestrial conditions."

The party now came over a long low ridge, and the mass of Ultra Vires rose from the desert ahead of them. The sun was near setting, and the black walls of the stronghold huddled sullenly under its crimson rays.

The Martians left them here, and Nuwell and Maya went on alone toward their goal. Nuwell expelled an audible sigh of relief.

"I'm glad we're free of those monsters," he said. "I don't understand how you could carry on a conversation with such creatures, Maya. It sounded like a series of animal grunts and cries to me. I caught an occasional word, like 'oxygen' and 'psychokinesis.' What were you talking about?"

"He was telling me about Goat Hennessey's experiments, and how they differed from the rebels' experiments before Goat came to Ultra Vires," answered Maya.

"That kind of talk serves no good purpose," said Nuwell irritably. "The rebel movement has been broken now, and there's no point in thinking about the illegal things they tried to do."

They came down the slope and approached the southern airlock of Ultra Vires. The airlock was still sealed. Nuwell activated it, and they went through it into the big building.

It was dark inside. Nuwell fumbled around a wall and found a light switch. He pressed it, but nothing happened.

"The electrical system isn't operating," he said. "We'll have to use our marsuit torches."

He switched on his flashlight. It cast a long beam down the dusty corridor. Far ahead of them, a small animal scurried across the faint light and vanished into the darkness.

Nuwell checked his atmosphere dial.

"The oxygen in here is all right," he said. "The air has been maintained, anyhow. We can take off our helmets." They took off the marshelmets and walked down the corridor. They checked each side door, looking for the communications room, but found only empty chambers or abandoned rooms in which books, papers and broken furniture were scattered in complete disorganization.

It took them nearly an hour to find the communications room. And there they met disappointment.

Ultra Vires' radio transmitter and receiver had been dismantled. There was nothing there but a jumble of broken tubes, discarded parts and bare wire ends dangling from the walls. Nothing but an overturned table and two bent metal chairs.

"That settles that," said Nuwell, more philosophically then Maya would have expected. "Our only hope is to find a groundcar."

That necessitated another search, but at last they found the motor pool. And there were three groundcars, all in various stages of breakdown or dismantlement.

"It looks like we'll have to walk, Nuwell," said Maya.

Nuwell shook his head.

"I checked the chart carefully," he said. "The oxygen supply of a marsuit won't take us either back to the Canfell Farm or to Ophir, even with extra tanks. We're just going to have to cannibalize two of these machines and repair us a groundcar."

"But, Nuwell, how long will that take?"

"I don't know," he admitted. "It looks like it may be quite a job. I expect it will take two or three weeks, but that's the only way we're going to get out of here."

He looked at her speculatively.

"It's a shame we aren't already married," he said. "This would provide us with a honeymoon, of a sort, out here by ourselves in the desert."

"Well, we aren't," she said flatly. "And we won't be until we get back to Mars City."

"That's true," he said. "Well, the only thing we can do for tonight is to have supper and find the rooms that Goat assigned us when we were here before. I hope he left some beds intact in those, or some of the other rooms. If not, we may have some uncomfortable nights ahead of us."

12

The two Dark Kensingtons and Happy Thurbelow walked along one of the pathways between the vats, Happy trailing a bit behind. Somewhere near them, they knew, Shadow accompanied them. The place was dim, with the moist dimness of a swamp. The source of the light that filtered through the faint mist and seemed to permeate the air was not discernible, and the roof of this underground world was lost in the darkness above them. The placid surface of the water gleamed vaguely in the vats they passed, and the pale-green tangle of vegetation rose above and around them, sometimes drooping over the paths like skinny arms that sought to detain them.

"What I don't understand," said Dark the younger, "is that our memories coincide exactly, up to a point which you say is a time twenty-five years ago. My memories are just as genuine as you say yours are; they aren't something someone told me, but real memories of things that happened to me, things I felt and did. If they're both genuine sets of memories, how can it be explained? Are we the same person, who was somehow split into two distinct individuals?"

"I can only guess at the explanation, but I have a theory," answered Old Beard. "You are much younger than I am. I would estimate that you're twenty-five years younger than I am. My memories are consecutive and complete: I remember not only the earlier things you say you remember, but the events of these past twenty-five years, without a break. You say you suffered a period of amnesia, and your next consecutive memory is of being with Martians in the Icaria Desert."

"That would appear to give you an advantage in claiming to be the real Dark Kensington," agreed Dark with a smile. "But, if you are, who am I? How is it that I remember being Dark Kensington?"

"It's entirely possible that, for some reason, my earlier memories were grafted onto you as your own," replied Old Beard. "I don't know how this would be done, perhaps through very deep and extensive hypnosis. The Martians, as well as we can tell anything about them at all, are experts in such mental fields, a relic of the ancient science they're legended to have had when their civilizations covered Mars.

"I worked with Martians very closely for long periods during the early days of the rebellion—the Phoenix, as you say they call it now—and they may very well have recorded my memory pattern through some means I don't know anything about and for reasons I can't imagine."

"That sounds reasonable," conceded Dark. "But that still leaves unanswered the questions: Who am I, and what's happened to my memories of the past twenty-five years?"

"I'm afraid I can't answer that," replied Old Beard.

In the dimness ahead of them, they discerned a group of nude Toughs approaching, swaggering down the path. They turned aside and found a recess in the vegetation in which they could wait until the Toughs passed and went on their way. The Toughs were aggressive, and insensately brutal, and a meeting with them could only mean trouble.

"Happy's explained the situation here, as well as he could, but I'm afraid it wasn't a very adequate explanation," said Dark as they huddled in the shadowed recess. "Could you tell me more about it, and explain how you happen to be here?"

"Happy is very intelligent, for a Jelly, but none of the Jellies are exceptionally bright," answered Old Beard, with a touch of affection in his voice. "I'll outline it to you as briefly as I can.

"As your memories–or transplanted memories–indicate, I was one of a group of Martian colonists who joined forces to work at what, at first, appeared to be a theoretical and fantastic project: the development of the ability to live under natural Martian conditions, without dependence on the regular importation of extremely expensive imports from Earth. As you know, this project very shortly began to lose its fantastic qualities and appear to be definitely within the realm of possible realization.

"Because of the differing background and orientation of those of us who attempted this project, two approaches were adopted. One, based on advancing terrestrial research into the field of extrasensory perception, was aimed at developing telepathic and telekinetic powers so that food, oxygen, machinery and other essentials could be teleported directly from Earth into the martian domes without dependence on the spacelines. The other, based on more orthodox science, was aimed at genetic development of a human type that could live *without* these importations, on native Martian food and in the Martian atmosphere.

"As you know, the government banned these experiments and we retreated into the desert to carry them on despite the ban. From what you tell me of the extent of your memories, what you do not know is the reason behind the ban, which we discovered–or, at least, I did–only after we had been betrayed and the government had raided and broken up our experimental colony.

"The spacelines, as one might have guessed, were responsible. They saw that the success of the experiments would destroy their lucrative business. These spacelines, led by the Mars Corporation, which later absorbed the others and gained a monopoly, brought political pressure to bear and got the project banned.

"I had heard reports that a great many of my colleagues escaped and formed a rebel organization that carried on the work secretly and illegally, but I was never able to learn details of it until you came and told me of the activities in which you have been engaged. You see, I haven't been out of these caves in a quarter of a century."

Shadow appeared at the recess to report to them that the Toughs had passed on. How he did it, Dark was unable to determine surely, for he could hear no words spoken. Either Shadow communicated by subtle gestures or by tones beyond Dark's powers of hearing, but both Old Beard and Happy seemed to understand him readily.

"How do you happen to be here, Old Beard?" asked Dark as they left the recess and resumed their progress down the walkways.

"I was captured when the government broke up the experimental groups," answered Old Beard. "I was the leader of the section of the experiments dealing with extrasensory perception, and, instead of executing me at once, they tried to persuade me to continue this work for the government along specific lines and under supervision. I refused, because I knew that anything I helped them develop would not be used for the benefit of the Martian colonists, but for greater profits for the spacelines.

"At last I was able to escape into these underground caverns where they grow food plants hydroponically and sell them to supplement the produce of the dome farms and the gardens in the dome cities. These caverns are extensive and, with the friendship and help of the Jellies, I've evaded discovery for twenty-five years."

"Just who and what are the Jellies?" asked Dark. "I haven't been able to get a very satisfactory answer to that question from Happy."

"They're human experimental animals," answered Old Beard. "The terrestrial food plants grown hydroponically and sold in the dome cities actually are a supplemental sideline to the real purpose of this place. Marscorp is conducting its own experiments here, with a crew of expert geneticists.

"What Marscorp is trying to do is to breed native Martian plants, that will grow in the open lowlands without expensive oxygenation and irrigation, that are not poisonous to humans and can be used for food. At the same time, they're approaching the problem from the other side, and the Jellies are men and women whose glandular structure has been altered in an effort to make their physiology more receptive to native Martian vegetation. If they succeed, of course, Marscorp has just as complete a monopoly over such a food supply as it does over imports from Earth, but at considerably less expense."

"And the Toughs?"

"They're human experimental animals, too, based on a different type of glandular alteration. They're neither as docile nor as intelligent as the Jellies, so they can't be used for slave labour as the Jellies can. About the only way they're ever used is as occasional goon squads to terrorize the Jellies and keep them in line."

"You've been here twenty-five years and have never been able to escape?" asked Dark incredulously.

"This place isn't guarded," replied Old Beard, with a wry smile. "They don't have to guard it. All they have to guard are the supply room where the marsuits are kept and the motor pool of groundcars. This place is in the middle of the Desert of Candor, and no one can live in the Martian desert without oxygen."

They came now to one of the walls of the underground cavern, and Old Beard led them suddenly into a fissure that was well concealed from the walkways by a tangled screen of vegetation. They stumbled along a narrow passageway for a few feet, and emerged into a rude shaft, around the walls of which a roughly-chiseled and steep stairway led upward into pitch darkness. Here Old Beard halted.

"When I told you there's no way of escape here, it was not that I haven't tried many times," he said to Dark.

"This shaft leads up into the walls of the structure above—above, although it is still underground—and I have been up there often at night. It has long been my hope that I might be able to get a marsuit or a groundcar and make my escape, but they are kept locked up and always guarded, against the Jellies and the Toughs.

"I want to take you up and give you an idea of the place now, and later perhaps you will have some ideas to contribute. Happy and Shadow will stay down here until we get back."

Old Beard mounted the steep steps slowly, and Dark followed at his heels. Although the bottom of the "well" was lighted with the same dim light as that which spread throughout the entire underground area, there was no light at all higher up, and they had to feel their way carefully lest they fall off the narrow steps.

At the top, Old Beard stopped and Dark bumped sharply into him.

"I'm going to move down the space between the walls," Old Beard whispered. "Hold onto my hand and follow me. But don't say anything or make any more noise than you can help, because anyone beyond the wall may be able to hear you."

They moved ahead. The way was very narrow, very dark and very difficult, and frequently was choked with ventilator pipes or tangles of wiring. They had gone some forty or fifty feet, when Old Beard stopped.

By Old Beard's movements, Dark knew he was working at something. Then a section of ventilator pipe came away from a ventilator grill, and faint light illuminated the space in which they crouched. In this dimness, Old Beard gestured to Dark to look through the ventilator.

Peering out, Dark saw that they were near the ceiling of a large, high-ceilinged room. In it, under glaring lights, a group of half a dozen white-clad men were working with knives and other instruments on the body of a man, either anaesthetized or dead, which lay on a surgical table.

Old Beard put his face against the grill next to Dark's, and the two men watched the scene below for a few moments. Then one of the men around the table raised his head, revealing a thin face, with watery blue eyes and a straggly goatee.

The two men inside the wall gasped as one man.

"*Father!*"

The single loud word was torn from Dark's throat without his volition, without his actually realizing he had spoken.

The heads of the men in the room jerked up at the cry, and they looked around and at each other, with puzzled expressions. Old Beard clapped a firm hand over Dark's mouth and hissed in his ear:

"Fool! Let's get out of here!"

As quietly as possible, they made their way back. Through the ventilator behind them came the murmur of querulous voices.

When they had climbed back down the stairs and, with Happy and Shadow, made their way back through the fissure, Old Beard fixed penetrating eyes on Dark and said:

"I told you to keep quiet up there! What was that exclamation all about?"

"It's something very strange," murmured Dark, his face thoughtful and bemused. "But you evidently recognized that man, too. Who is he?"

"Yes, I know him very well," answered Old Beard, with deep bitterness in his tone. "That's Goat Hennessey. But that's the first time I've seen him in twenty-five years. He must have just come here recently."

"Goat Hennessey? I heard of him when I was in Mars City."

"Goat Hennessey was one of my most trusted friends," said Old Beard. "If you bear my earlier memories, I'm surprised you didn't recognize him as Goat Hennessey, too."

"I recognized him as someone else," said Dark in a low voice.

"We worked together," went on Old Beard. "I was a leader in the effort to solve our problem through extrasensory perception, and he was the major scientist in the group attempting to solve it by genetic change. We worked together and we went into the desert together with the others when the government banned our experiments.

"But Goat was the man who sold out. He betrayed us to the government–for what price I don't know. And when government agents raided us and broke up our organization and captured me, Goat Hennessey kidnapped my young and pregnant wife, and I never saw her again.

"I'm glad Goat Hennessey is here, because now I can get to him. And when I can reach him, I'm going to kill him. I'd like to kill him as slowly and painfully as he killed the heart inside of me!"

As Old Beard spoke these last words, his face was tense, his fists clenched and a somber fire burned in his pale eyes. Then, slowly, the fire died out and he turned his eyes, once more cool and rational, a little quizzical, on Dark.

"Didn't you call him 'father'?" he asked.

"Yes," said Dark in a low voice. "But I'd rather not talk about it right now."

He looked at Old Beard, and seemed to be ridding himself, with an effort, of a deep introversion.

"There's one thing that I've remembered as a result of seeing Goat Hennessey," said Dark in a firmer voice. "This place isn't too far from a place in the Xanthe Desert where Goat conducted some significant experiments. If he left any of his records there–and I'm thinking of some in particular–they might go a long way toward solving the problem we've all be working on for so long. So now I know what to do next: I'm going to Ultra Vires."

Old Beard smiled sadly.

"Have you forgotten we can't get out of this place?" he reminded. "We can't get at either the marsuits or the groundcars."

It was Dark's turn to smile.

"I believe you said there aren't any guards on the airlocks to stop one from walking out at night?" he said.

"That's true, but—"

"There's something you don't know," continued Dark. "You were wondering at the basis of the regenerative power that permitted me to revive here after being shot in the stomach with a heatgun. I don't know what it is, but whatever it is, it's something that also permits me to live without oxygen.

"Happy can testify that I was fully alive and conscious underwater. I discovered, before I was shot, that I can operate just as well outside, in the Martian atmosphere, without a helmet. And that's why Goat's records may solve our problem.

"So tonight I'll leave this place and go to Ultra Vires. If there are any marsuits and groundcars left there, I'll come back here with them, and you and Happy and Shadow can escape with me. If not, you may have to wait a while longer.

"But I'll be back!"

13

Brute Hennessey plodded westward through the Xanthe Desert, naked, wearing no marsuit, his head bare to the thin, oxygen-poor Martian air. The two small moons shone in the star-spangled sky above the lone figure, casting fantastic shadows on the sands. But this was not the stupid, shambling Brute Hennessey of a few months past. He walked surely and proudly, and the light of intelligence shone in his eyes.

He called himself, now, Dark Kensington.

Dark's muscular body had not regained, quite, the firmness and tone it had had before he was shot down at Solis Lacus, but he had recovered greatly from the bloated flabbiness of a few days ago. Most of that had been water in his tissues, and resumption of normal physical activity had wrung it out in short order.

As he plodded through the Martian night toward Ultra Vires, Dark was remembering, with something of awe, that emotional explosion within him that had occurred on his first sight of Goat Hennessey at the Canfell Hydroponic Farm. It was this sudden, overwhelming recognition that had wrung from his lips the cry: "*Father!*"

In that moment, memory had returned with terrible impact and he had been overwhelmed by the re-experience of those moments when he had stood before the man he admired and loved as his father and had seen the bitter realization of rejection by that man written with the point of a knife.

Now he remembered it all. He remembered his childhood at Ultra Vires, he remembered Adam and their experiences together, he remembered their treks through the desert at Goat Hennessey's command, he remembered his slaying of Adam and his acceptance of death at Goat's hands. He remembered that he, Dark Kensington, was Brute Hennessey, somehow brought to life once before in the Icaria Desert even as he had himself regained life a second time in the vats of the Canfell Hydroponic Farm.

So Goat Hennessey was his father, apparently. And Old Beard, the real Dark Kensington, vowed vengeance on Goat. Dark was able to view this with equanimity. He no longer felt any admiration or affection for Goat, whatever relationship might exist between them.

But, since he was Brute Hennessey and thus not old enough to be the real Dark Kensington, how and why had he acquired the memories of Dark Kensington? That question remained unanswered.

Phobos was setting for the first time that night when Dark reached the great hulk of Ultra Vires, manipulated one of the airlocks and entered its dark corridors. There was no light, and a test of the light switch proved that the electrical system was no longer operating. But Dark knew every inch of this place from early childhood. He felt his way through the pitch darkness to Goat Hennessey's old bedroom.

Probing about in the darkness, he discovered that Goat's bed was still supplied with mattress and crumpled blankets. This surprised him somewhat, as any item of cloth on Mars had to be imported from Earth and was far too valuable to abandon. But, apparently, these things had been left temporarily in Goat's abandonment of Ultra Vires and would be picked up by truck later.

Deriving a certain humorous satisfaction from taking over the master's chamber, Dark curled up on Goat's bed and went to sleep.

He awoke the next morning with the glare of the desert sunlight reflected into the room. He arose, stretched and yawned. The room was a mess. Goat had left the bed clothing intact, but he had turned everything else upside down in packing his personal effects to leave the place.

There was still water in the reservoir, and Ultra Vires' plumbing system was still in operation. Dark bathed. He felt ruefully at the thick stubble of beard that had overgrown his face in the past few days, but Goat had left no shaving equipment behind.

Dark made his way down to the big kitchen. There were supplies of canned food there, and he found utensils and ate. He was hungry, but not ravenous, and this surprised him a little, because he had had no food since he started out afoot from the Canfell Hydroponic Farm, four nights ago. But he was no hungrier than he would normally be after a night's sleep.

As he ate, his eye fell on dishes stacked beside the sink. He was startled to notice that water still sparkled on them.

He arose and checked them. Yes, they were still wet.

There were remnants of fresh food in the garbage can.

People, here? Camping out? Or, more likely, someone passing through the desert who had taken shelter here for the night? But he thought he would have heard the roar of a groundcar leaving.

Thoughtfully, Dark finished his breakfast. It occurred to him that perhaps some members of the Phoenix had taken refuge here after fleeing Mars City. But most of them did not even know of the existence of Ultra Vires, much less its location.

At any rate, there was no reason to assume that anyone who happened to be here would be unfriendly to him, in case they met by chance. He saw no reason to worry about it.

Finishing breakfast, Dark went down to the storeroom and picked out three marsuits, for Old Beard, Happy and Shadow. There was a large-sized suit there that he thought might accommodate Happy's bulk, but he wondered how Shadow, with his flat build, was going to manage one.

Nakedness felt quite natural to Dark, especially since he remembered his identity as Brute, but it occurred to him that it would look peculiar to anyone he might meet before leaving Ultra Vires—or, for that matter, on his way back to the Canfell Hydroponic Farm. So he donned a marsuit himself, leaving off the helmet.

Carrying the other three marsuits, he went down the corridor to the motor pool.

Dark remembered that Goat had always kept four groundcars on hand. There were three here now, all in advanced stages of dismantlement.

At one of them, a small figure in black tunic and loose trousers was bending over, head and arms plunged into the bowels of the engine.

Dark hesitated. He had found his intruder, perhaps a traveler who had run into engine trouble in the desert and had fortuitously been near enough to take shelter here while making repairs. But, again, there was no reason to anticipate unfriendliness.

Carrying his marsuits, Dark walked up to the groundcar, overhearing a muffled bit of profanity as he approached. The unfortunate mechanic evidently heard his footsteps, because he was greeted with:

"I wish to Phobos you'd stay down here and *try* to help me, instead of spending all your time snooping around this deserted shack!"

The voice was muffled, but it was definitely feminine and definitely irritated. Dark grinned and replied drolly:

"I'm sorry, but this is the first time you've asked me to help you."

With an audible gasp, the woman disentangled herself, in dangerous haste, from the groundcar engine and faced Dark.

They stared at each other, in mutual shocked recognition.

There was Dark Kensington, bearded, his arms full of marsuits, and there was Maya Cara Nome, sleeves rolled up, her lovely face streaked with grease. Dark's jaw dropped. Maya's lips formed a round, astonished O. Then, with a squeal, she hurled herself on him, throwing her arms around his neck. Dark staggered back, overwhelmed by marsuits, an abundance of wriggling femininity and a babble of happy and-completely unintelligible words gushed against his bearded cheek.

He managed to disentangle himself by the dual process of dropping the marsuits and holding Maya forcibly at arm's length. She gazed up into his face, her own awed and radiant, and was able to reduce her own words to connected sentences.

"You're not here," she said positively. "You can't be here. You're dead. I saw you killed. You must be one of the ghosts of Ultra Vires."

She wriggled free and threw her arms around his neck again, announcing happily, "But you're a solid, *comfortable* ghost, and I love you!"

Again, Dark managed to get her at arm's length and looked down seriously into her face.

"Did I hear you correctly?" he asked soberly. "Did you say you love me?"

"I did. And I mean it. Oh, Dark, how I mean it!"

He pulled her to him. He kissed her gravely. Then he held her close in his arms, while she rested her head contentedly against his shoulder.

"What," he asked at last, "are you doing here, tinkering with a groundcar?"

"Nuwell and I were on our way to Mars City by helicopter, when it failed and crashed," she explained. "This was the only place near enough for us to make it afoot, and the marsuit radios don't have the range to call for help. We've been here more than two weeks now, trying to repair these groundcars."

She looked at the machine she had been working on and shook her head ruefully.

"I don't think any of them can be fixed," she said. "Nuwell, it turns out, doesn't know a damn thing about machinery, but I was taught a good deal about mechanics when I was trained as a terrestrial agent. Even with three groundcars to supply parts, there are some things missing that I don't think I can jury-rig substitutes for."

She turned back to Dark.

"But you're dead!" she exclaimed. "I know you are, because we carried your body with us to the Canfell Hydroponic Farm. How in space can you be here, alive and kissing, when you made such a beautiful corpse?"

Dark explained the circumstances to her; how he had awakened in the vat, how he had been able to breathe underwater, how the sight of Goat Hennessey had revived in him the memory of his identity as Brute, how he had been able to walk across the desert without a marsuit.

"If you're Brute Hennessey, I know why you aren't dead," she said when he had finished. "We fell in with a party of Martians on our way here, and they told me about certain embryonic changes they made on you and Adam before Goat kidnapped your mothers and brought them to Ultra Vires. Qril—he's the Martian I talked to—said that these alterations not only permit you to live in a free Martian environment, but give you extraordinary regenerative powers."

"They must be extraordinary, if they permit me to come to life again after being stabbed in the heart and having my belly burned out with a heatgun," observed Dark.

"That's because your tissues aren't dependent on oxygen-carbon combustion," explained Maya. "According to Qril, when oxygen is no longer available to you, your cells utilize direct solar energy. That would prevent your tissues from dying while the damaged area of your body is under repair."

She looked at him in sudden awed realization.

"It would seem, darling, that you're virtually indestructible!" she said.

Dark laughed.

"Perhaps so," he said. "But I don't hanker to experiment along those lines any more than necessary. Dying is a very unpleasant experience, even if I do come to life again."

"Oh, Dark," said Maya, remembering. "I'd like for Qril to see you, and maybe he'll give us some more information. They came back here three days ago and, for some reason, have just been hanging around outside, under the walls. Let me get on a marsuit, and I'll take you to him."

"Here, put on one of these," suggested Dark, picking up the one he had selected for Old Beard.

Maya wriggled into it. The Martians, she said, were on the other side of Ultra Vires, so they left the motor pool and walked down one of the long corridors together, Maya clinging to Dark's arm with one hand and carrying her marshelmet under her other arm.

They were halfway across the big building when Nuwell Eli appeared around a corner about thirty feet ahead of them. He stopped, staring, at the sight of Maya's companion.

"Maya," he began, as they neared him. "Who ...?"

Then he recognized Dark.

With a terrified yelp, Nuwell turned and raced back down the side corridor at top speed. They heard the clack-clack of his heels on the stone floor, fading in the distance.

Dark and Maya stopped and looked at each other.

"It must have been quite a shock to him, too, to see you risen from the dead," she said. "I don't believe he's as happy to see you as I was, Dark."

"No, his joy seemed considerably mitigated," replied Dark gravely. "But, Maya, this raises a rather serious question which hadn't occurred to me before, in the happiness of our reunion."

"What's that, darling?"

"You're a terrestrial agent and, as such, you put me under arrest. It's true, you tried to free me later. But didn't you tell me that night that you were engaged to marry this man, Nuwell Eli?"

"Yes," she admitted in a small voice. "But—"

"I haven't had the pleasure of meeting the gentleman before," continued Dark, still in the same grave tone. "But you and he were going back to Mars City together, and, for some reason, it occurs to me that you and he planned to be married as soon as you could get there."

Maya was somewhat stunned at this evidence of mind reading.

"That's true," she said in a very small voice.

"Now," said Dark, "you tell me that you love me. You must admit that the question raised by this is rather serious. Does this declaration of love—which, I assure you, is reciprocated completely—imply a radical change in your past course of action? Or, since you're still a terrestrial agent, can I expect to be arrested again as a preliminary to your joining Mr. Eli in the holy state of matrimony?"

Maya looked up into his face, and burst out laughing.

"I may have put it jokingly," protested Dark, a little taken aback, "but I'm serious, Maya."

"I know you are!" she giggled. "That's what makes it so funny. Answering you in the same vein, Mr. Kensington, I don't intend to put you in double jeopardy!"

Dark raised his eyebrows quizzically.

"I arrested you and you were killed resisting arrest," she explained mischievously. "I've discharged that duty as a terrestrial agent, so I don't think I'm either required or entitled to arrest you again. And as for the other, well, I am a little sorry for Nuwell, but I do love you, and I won't marry Nuwell, since you're alive. But I can't marry you, Dark."

Dark was stunned at this.

"Why not, Maya? You mean, because you're a terrestrial agent?"

"No, it isn't that. I'm planning to resign as an agent, as soon as I get back to Mars City, and that wouldn't stop me, anyway. The reason I can't marry you is simply that you haven't asked me."

Dark laughed, a rollicking, relieved laugh, and swept her into his arms.

"Maya, darling, I ask you now!" he exclaimed. "Will you marry me?"

"Yes, Dark," she answered demurely.

She leaned back in the circle of his arms and looked up into his face, seriously.

"Whither thou goest, I will go," she said, very quietly. "If you're a rebel, Dark, I'll be a rebel, too. I want to be with you, and help you in whatever you do."

14

Dark and Maya sat with their backs against the wall of Ultra Vires, and Qril squatted before them, towering huge above them. A little distance away the other three Martians were grouped, playing some sort of game, doing some sort of work or participating in some sort of joint demonstration. Dark could not be sure which.

Qril boomed out a long, rolling sentence and Maya broke into laughter. She turned to Dark and translated:

"He said he didn't understand why I'm wearing a helmet, when you aren't. I explained that I have to wear a helmet to breathe, and he said that, since you and I are alike, it appears that we'd dress alike. So you see, darling, even the Martians recognize that we're made for each other."

Dark shook his head in wonderment.

"No human has ever been able to figure out Martian thinking processes, and I doubt that one ever will," he remarked. "This is the Martian who explained to you the physiological structure that permits me to live without oxygen, and yet he asks a question like that!"

"There's one thing that puzzles me," said Maya curiously. "Without a helmet, you can't use your marsuit heater, and you said you walked here naked. But the temperature out here right now is well below freezing. Aren't you cold?"

"No," answered Dark. "I get cold in temperatures that are uncomfortable to anyone else when I'm in a dome or a building and breathing. But out here, when I'm not breathing, I'm aware of temperature changes but they don't cause me any discomfort. It must be that switching to direct utilization of solar power alters my reactions to temperature."

"Well," said Maya, "I can understand that utilization of solar power when you're in the sunshine. But how can you keep operating when you're in shadow, or at night, and not breathing?"

"I don't know. Maybe Qril does."

Maya asked the Martian, and relayed his answer to Dark:

"Qril says that you store excess energy in the tissues, very much as the Martians store oxygen. In a sense, direct sunlight's your generator, and it charges your batteries for power when it isn't operating. Now, Dark, why don't you ask him anything you want to know about your origin, and I'll act as translator."

"All right," agreed Dark. "But first, it was among Martians that I awoke when I returned to life the first time in the Icaria Desert. That's pretty far away, but I understand Martians have a weird sort of sympathetic communication among themselves. Does he know anything about how I got there?"

Maya talked with Qril and translated:

"Qril is one of the Martians I saw come by here and pick up your body the morning after Goat killed you and threw your body out in the desert. Qril says they recognized you from your genetic pattern—and don't ask me how they did this!—as being the one they had completed embryonic alteration on years before, so they picked you up and took you with them to give you a chance to regenerate and revive."

"But how and why did I turn up after my revival with Dark Kensington's memories?"

"He says they gave you a memory pattern by a deep telepathic process," answered Maya after talking with Qril, "because your memory pattern as Brute was of no value to you in meeting a new environment. It seems that there was some blockage in the operation of your brain as Brute, because of a slight fault in the embryonic alteration, and they corrected that before you revived."

"But why Dark Kensington's memory pattern?" asked Dark. "It turned out to be a valuable one for me, but I've met the real Dark Kensington since then, and he's a much older man. Why did they choose his memory pattern?"

Maya talked with Qril.

"He says names mean very little to them," she said then. "That's something I learned as a child: that Martians often interchange their names, and the names evidently refer to a state of experience and being rather than to a specific individual. But he says that the memory pattern they chose to give you was that of your father!"

Dark stared at her, stunned.

"Then," he said slowly, "Old Beard is my father. I should have known! I think I felt it."

"I'm not surprised if you did," said Maya. "From what Qril tells me, Dark, this prenatal alteration they performed on you gave you even more extensive powers than we realized. He says that you have extraordinary extrasensory ability, if you would only make an effort to use it."

"Oh, I do, do I?" murmured Dark thoughtfully.

He looked over at the other Martians, seated in a circle in the morning sunshine. They were taking turns tossing some small polygons, and evidently the objective of whatever they were doing lay in the way the polygons fell.

Dark felt a sudden surge of power in his brain. He concentrated it, he focused it, and one of the polygons rose slowly from the ground and drifted into the air above the Martians' heads.

Dark could feel the strength that went out and raised the polygon, like an invisible extension of himself. Then he felt another force seize the polygon, and it was drawn back firmly and without hesitation to its former place.

Dark turned his head back to look into Qril's huge eyes, and at once he was in mental contact with the Martian.

Qril was laughing at him. There was no change of expression on Qril's face, but in his mind was the atmosphere of high humor. Qril's thoughts came to him without words, in no language, silently but clearly:

You have not practised your power. Experience will be necessary before you can compete with the simplest effort of one of our race.

Dark turned to Maya.

"He's right," said Dark. "I do have extrasensory powers, but they'll need some development."

"I know," said Maya. "The telepathic voltage in the atmosphere must be very high right now, because even I sensed your effort in lifting that object, and I understood Qril's communication to you."

Maya and Dark took their leave of Qril, and went back into Ultra Vires. As they did so, Qril and the other Martians arose and began to drift away into the desert, as though they had had a mission in staying here, which was now accomplished.

"I hope you know something about mechanics," said Maya as they walked down the corridor together. "Because if you don't, it looks like we're stuck here for a while. At least I am, unless you can run one of these groundcars with psychokinetic power."

"No, apparently I'm not that good at it yet," said Dark. "Maybe I could teleport in any parts you need. No wait! I just remembered something! Come with me."

They turned off into a side corridor, found stairs and climbed to the top floor of the building. There they followed another corridor until Dark stopped and opened a door.

It was the door to a small airlock. Dark led Maya through it into a huge room.

A helicopter stood in its center.

"Goat *did* leave it here!" exclaimed Dark joyfully. "I'd forgotten that he had this. He must have just packed the most necessary things when he left the place, planning to send trucks and a crew back and clean it out later at his leisure. Now, if this copter's only in good flying shape, we're set."

He checked the machine over. Everything was in order.

"How do we get it out of here?" asked Maya curiously, looking around the room. "That little airlock's too small for a copter to go through it."

"The roof rolls back," said Dark. "Put on your helmet, and I'll show you."

Maya donned her marshelmet. Dark went to the wall and pulled a switch. Nothing happened.

"I forgot," he said. "The electricity's off. Well, let's try something."

Dark concentrated his mind intensely on the movable ceiling. For a moment, there was resistance, then, very slowly, it began to open. A crack appeared in its center, and the air of the room hissed out with the swish of a minor tempest. After that, it was easier. The crack widened swiftly, and the roof rolled back to the walls, leaving the room open to the heavens.

"All we have to do now is to climb into it and go," said Dark with satisfaction. "You fill the fuel tanks, and I'll run down to the motor pool and pick up those other two marsuits. One of them is for my friend Happy, who is very fat, and he couldn't wear either of the emergency suits in the copter."

Maya uncoiled the hose from one of the fuel drums in the room and poked it into the copter's tank. Dark left the room, walked down the corridor and descended the stairs.

He made his way to the motor pool. Maya was wearing one of the three marsuits he had brought down, but the other two were still lying on the floor. He picked them up and started back.

He was walking down the first floor corridor, carrying the marsuits, when there crashed in on his mind a terrifying, silent scream:

Help!

Dark stopped, appalled. It took him a moment to realize that he was still standing in the corridor. It took him a moment to realize that he actually had heard nothing.

The corridor stretched away ahead of him, dim and dusty. There was no movement in it, no sound. It was utterly silent. He stood there, in a dim, dusty corridor, in waiting silence, holding two marsuits under his arms.

Help!

It was a cry that shrieked in his mind, reverberated in his mind, touching nothing around him, touching not the silent corridor.

Maya!

Dark's mind went out to her, rode up on swift wings to the room above where she had waited for his return.

He was there, in that room, and there was the helicopter. There was no Maya there.

But there were figures in the copter, moving.

He was in the copter, and there was Maya, struggling and writhing, as Nuwell Eli, in a furious concentration of savage energy, bound her into one of its seats with a length of rope.

Dark touched her mind, and her mind grasped his, desperately.

Dark, he followed us up here, and hid until you left. He crept up behind me and seized me. Hurry, Dark, he's taking me away!

Hurry? Down those corridors, up those steps, when Nuwell already was sliding into the pilot's seat of the copter?

Frantically, Dark grasped at his only chance of reaching her in time. Teleportation.

He clamped down with his mind on himself. With a frenzied burst of strength, he sought to lift himself bodily, to be there in the copter with them. He put every ounce of energy he possessed into the effort.

And he failed.

He was standing in the dim, dusty corridor, two marsuits under his arm, straining futilely toward a place he could not reach. And now he actually heard, with his ears, the muted vibration above him as the copter's engines roared to life.

Dark started running.

He dropped the marsuits, and ran down the corridor. He leaped up the stairs, two and three at a time. Breathless, his heart pounding, he staggered down the upper corridor and impatiently went through the seemingly interminable process of negotiating the airlock.

He emerged into the big room.

It was empty.

The ceiling was open to the Martian sky. The sunlight poured into the roofless room.

In the sky, a small, teetering object rose and moved away from Ultra Vires, its blades whirring a sparkling circle in the thin air.

Dark reached out to it with his mind, and again he was in the copter. Nuwell sat tensely at the controls, guiding it. Maya was in the other seat, her arms bound down by her sides, her expression agonized.

Nuwell was unaware of Dark's mental presence. Maya sensed it and her mind turned toward him.

Dark, Dark, what can we do? I should have been watching for him. I should have known, after he saw us together, that he would do something.

Dark: *It was my fault, Maya. I shouldn't have left you alone. I just didn't consider him a factor to be reckoned with, and I should have known better.*

Maya: *What can we do?*

Nuwell turned to Maya, and his face was bitter and sullen. His brown eyes were flat with anger.

"You treacherous witch, I should have known better than to trust you after that trick of trying to help Kensington escape. I wanted to give you a chance, because I thought that, with him dead, you might have recovered from your madness," he said.

A change came over his face: a mixture of fear, disbelief and utter lack of comprehension.

"He *was* dead," said Nuwell, a hysterical note underlying his tone. "I saw him. You saw him dead, too, didn't you, Maya? How could he be back there with you?"

Maya's only answer was a defiant smile.

"There's some explanation for this," said Nuwell, more positively. "I don't know what it is, but I'll find it. That man back there isn't Dark Kensington, because Kensington's dead. Maya, I promise you, I'm going to find out what the answer is, but first I'm going to make sure that you don't cause me any more trouble."

Dark touched Maya's mind.

Maya, I'm going to try something here.

He moved back. He was outside the copter, near it, keeping pace with it as it flew. It was tilted slightly forward, falling forward through the sky at the pull of its blades.

Dark seized the copter with his mind. He tried to drag it back.

It hesitated. It quivered. Then it jerked forward and went on. He felt his mental grasp slipping from it.

Suddenly he was completely in the big room in Ultra Vires, the room with its roof open to the sky. He could no longer touch the copter. He could no longer be in it. He could no longer touch Maya's mind.

He tried. He reached out again. But he failed. He was where he was.

He realized he was almost exhausted. The tremendous drain of his efforts on his energy told on him at last. He no longer had the strength to try any more, and Nuwell and Maya were gone away from him into the Martian sky.

Wearily, he turned back and went through the airlock, down the corridor and down the stairs.

There was nothing more he could do now. Nuwell undoubtedly would take Maya to Mars City. And then? Maya would refuse to marry Nuwell now, and Dark doubted that Nuwell could force her. What Nuwell would do with her, he did not know. Probably some sort of confinement, eventually perhaps a trial. But Nuwell had no ground or reason to do her any real harm.

He would have to try to get to Maya as soon as he could, and that meant intensification of his efforts. But there was only one course he could hope to follow successfully, and that was the course he had planned when he started out for Ultra Vires.

Only now he *could* speed it up.

He had to have some rest. Then he would pick up three marsuits and walk back across the desert to the Canfell Hydroponic Farm.

15

Dark walked across the desert toward the Canfell Hydroponic Farm.

He had discarded the marsuit he had been wearing, and substituted for it a light loincloth torn from one of Goat Hennessey's sheets. This reverse reaction, in a temperature that would be uncomfortably chilly for a fully clothed man and descended far below zero at night, resulted from his recognition that he gained a tremendously greater direct influx of energy from the total exposure of his skin to the sunlight. He could feel the energy penetrating his flesh, building up in him. And, with this energy, the low temperature did not bother him.

Behind him, by a rope, he dragged a little two-wheeled cart he had constructed from groundcar parts. It rolled and bumped over the sandy terrain, containing all the marsuits and all the seven heatguns that he had been able to find at Ultra Vires.

It also contained a supply of water, in cans. Dark had found that, while he was operating directly on solar energy, he did not need food at all and he did not need as much water as he did under ordinary circumstances. He probably could have survived two weeks without any water at all. But some water did make him much more efficient. His independence of food and oxygen did not prevent the slow dessication if his tissues in the dry Martian air.

As he walked, only part of his mind was devoted to the routine task of moving across the desert. The remainder of it was free of the limitation of distance, touching and interacting with the minds of three other men.

These men were members of the Phoenix. At the Childress Barber College, they had been among the instructors, struggling to develop the ESP potentialities of their students so that a psychic community of purpose and action might be developed toward the goal of teleporting materials from Earth to Mars.

These were the men whose ability at telepathy and psychokinesis had been most fully developed, to the point of practical demonstration. Now, newly aware of the extent of his own inner powers, Dark had conceived a bold plan of action to which these men's comparable abilities was a necessary contribution.

There were three of them: Mantar Falusaine at Hesperidum, Pietro Corrallani at Mars City and Cheng I K'an at Ophir. Among them, by a vast intangible network of communication, they discussed strategy and the situation on which it was based.

Mantar: *We knew of the existence of the Canfell Hydroponic Farm. It was on our charts as a Marscorp industry, supported by the government. But we thought it was only an industry, producing food. We did not know it was an experimental center.*

Cheng: *We did not know Marscorp was conducting genetic experiments at all, except those of Goat Hennessey. We kept a casual observation on Goat's work. Our intention was that, if he ever succeeded completely in what he was trying to do, we would make a fast raid with a task force and appropriate his work to our own purposes.*

Dark chuckled.

Dark: *That would have dismayed Marscorp! But it appears that, as things have developed, this sort of raid must be directed now at the Canfell Hydroponic Farm, to free my father and the Marscorp slaves there. Old Beard is, after all, the real leader of the Phoenix. If we succeed in kidnapping Goat, we can put him to work for us, but that is not the primary objective.*

Pietro: *Do you plan to take over the Canfell Hydroponic Farm, and make it our base of operation?*

Dark: *No. When we attack the Farm, they will radio Mars City for help and we don't possess the force to fight off an all-out government counterattack. I have been in communication with a Martian friend, Qril, and I am informed that the domes in the Icaria Desert, which were used by the original rebels a quarter of a century ago, are still usable, although they will have to be supplied with oxygen, food and water. I intend for the Phoenix to congregate there and utilize the help of the Martians in carrying out the embryonic changes which will make your children and mine as I am. A new race, capable of living in the natural Martian environment.*

Pietro: *Will these characteristics of which you speak be inherited, or must the embryonic changes be made in each generation?*

Dark: *They will be inherited, because they are changes of the genetic structure. The changes will have to be made on each individual embryo of your children, but their children will be born with these qualities naturally.*

Cheng: *What are your instructions?*

Dark: *How many Phoenix are at each of your places?*

Cheng: *Twelve at Ophir.*

Mantar: *I would have to count. About twice that many at Hesperidum.*

Pietro: *About seventy-five here, as well as the wives of most of the Phoenix who are married.*

Dark: *Seventy-five! That's more than we had in school!*

Pietro: *Don't forget that the school was there for a long time before you came, and it had many graduates. The government captured between a third and a half of us who were in the school at that time, but there are still probably three to four hundred Phoenix scattered about Mars.*

Dark: *Where are the other three instructors, whom I was unable to contact with this telepathic call?*

Pietro: *They are at Charax, Nuba and Ismenius. Their telepathic powers are not as well developed as ours, and they would not hear you unless they were expecting the call.*

Dark: *Cheng, I thought your group was to go to Regina.*

Cheng: *It was, but the Regina airlocks were more effectively blockaded to us than at the other cities. Those who went to the other cities, except those who were caught, had identification establishing them as legitimate residents of those cities. Regina has a peculiar social structure which makes this virtually impossible, except for the Phoenix who are already there and have been for a long time. We thought of stopping at Zur, but there were no arrangements to care for us there. We went to a dome farm operated by a friend of the Phoenix in Pandorae Fretum, and stayed there until we could trickle gradually into Ophir.*

Dark: *You had quite an odyssey. Cheng, I want you to bring your twelve in groundcars, with what weapons you can get, and attack the Canfell Hydroponic Farm. I'll try to break it open from inside.*

Pietro: *Shall I bring my group from Mars City as reinforcements?*

Dark: *No, twelve will be enough, and the conquest of the farm will depend on speed. Before you can get there with your group by groundcar, the government will have a well-armed force there by jet. I want you to load trucks with supplies, gather all the wives and go straight to the Icaria Desert to establish our colony. I'll direct you telepathically when you reach Icaria, if we aren't already there. Cut across the deserts and lowlands, and stay away from the roads and cities.*

Pietro: *Very well. But we'll have to leave the city vehicle by vehicle, and rendezvous somewhere in the lowland. It will take some time.*

Dark: *Whatever is necessary. Do you know where the Chief is?*

Pietro: *He's here in jail in Mars City. His trial is due in twenty days, and we had planned to rescue him sometime during the trial.*

Dark: *Leave a few good men there to rescue him as soon as you've cleared Mars City and are on the way to Icaria. Has Nuwell Eli gotten back to Mars City yet?*

Pietro: *I don't know. We can find out.*

Dark: *He has Maya Cara Nome with him. She's the girl who was the secretary at the barber college when it was raided, and she's one of the Phoenix now. I want her rescued, at the same time, if possible. If not, I'll go to Mars City and do it myself later, but I want to get all of you cleared of the city first.*

Mantar: *What do you want me to do?*

Dark: *The most difficult thing of all. I want you to stay in Hesperidum, and send out all the Phoenix you have with you to contact those in other Martian cities. They are to rendezvous at Hesperidum, and then you will gather supplies and form another caravan to join the rest of us in Icaria.*

Cheng: *When shall I move out?*

Dark: *As soon as you can gather your men and material together. But stay out of sight of the farm and don't attack until you hear from me. I should be there within the next forty-eight hours.*

The instructions given, the telepathic conference faded out, and Dark was a solitary man plodding across the desert, pulling a loaded cart behind him.

He came in sight of the Canfell Hydroponic Farm in just about the time that he had predicted to Cheng, but waited until nightfall to approach it. Phobos was abroad in the east at sunset, so Dark waited a little longer, until the nearer moon plunged beneath the eastern horizon. Deimos was not in the sky this night, and Phobos' disappearance left it near pitch-dark.

Dark moved across the starlit desert, pulling his cart, to the walls of the farm. The farm was not a massive, sprawling fortress like Ultra Vires, because most of it was underground. The upper floor, in which Happy's "Masters" lived and worked, was just below the ground level and the underground vats were below it, extending considerably beyond it in all directions. The only parts of the farm that projected above ground were its four entrances, small buildings of white stone, each with its own airlock.

Dark went through the airlock of the nearest one. These entrance buildings were the barracks of the Toughs, in which they slept at night, secure from the possibility of escape because no marsuits were available to them. Dark had moved quietly through a barracks of sleeping Toughs the night he had left the farm for Ultra Vires, but this time he had his cart with him.

There was no alternative but a bold course. Spearing the light of an electric torch before him, he walked down the aisle toward the barred gate leading into the regions below, pulling the metal-wheeled cart across the stone floor behind him.

Its clatter brought the whole barracks awake. On all sides of him arose an angry growling and shouting, an upsurge from many throats of the animal noises that were the Toughs' nearest approach to human language. Dark moved forward steadily, keeping a telepathic "radar" out to warn him of any impending attack.

The very boldness of his action paid off. Its openness apparently convinced the Toughs that this was merely another, unusually noisy case of one of the Masters returning to the farm at night–as Dark sensed had occurred often before. Dark was not molested.

The barred gate had no controls on this side. Dark operated it psychokinetically. It raised slowly, he pulled his cart through, and he lowered it behind him and went on down the ramp into the underground cavern.

He went straight to Old Beard's hiding place, and awoke him. Old Beard greeted him joyously.

"I was afraid something had happened to you, you were gone so long," said Old Beard.

"I had to walk back," said Dark. "None of the groundcars at Ultra Vires was in operating condition."

"Then there's no chance of the rest of us escaping," said Old Beard disappointedly. "We can't get at the groundcars here, and the marsuits you brought won't help. The oxygen supply of a marsuit isn't adequate to take us from here to the nearest civilization."

"I think we can get to the groundcars," answered Dark confidently. "I brought heatguns, as well as marsuits. Besides, I have a larger plan now than merely escape."

He related to Old Beard all the things that had happened, including the fact that Old Beard was his father.

"I am very happy," said Old Beard simply, tears in his pale eyes. "I liked you very much from the first, Dark, and I'm glad that you can bear the name of Dark Kensington rightfully."

When Dark told him of the plan for the conquest of the farm, Old Beard stroked his beard thoughtfully.

"I'm afraid that the attack from within will depend largely on you and me, although Shadow probably will be able to help effectively," said Old Beard. "The Jellies aren't very aggressive and, even with a few heatguns, I'm afraid they won't be of much use."

"How about the Toughs?"

"The Toughs would be fine, if you want to wipe out all the Masters and all the Jellies, and possibly us, too. They're vicious and unintelligent, and they can't be disciplined or depended upon."

"With the attack from the outside timed right, I think the three of us can handle it," said Dark. "How many of the Masters are there?"

"Only ten," answered Old Beard. "And they aren't soldiers, but scientists. But they do have weapons, and they know how to handle them. They have to, in order to keep the Toughs from getting out of line."

"Perhaps we can whip the Jellies up to the point of causing a good deal of initial trouble and confusion, and then the three of us move in at the proper moment after the attack from outside is under way," said Dark. "We might even turn the Toughs loose on them, without weapons."

Old Beard gave him a steady gaze from beneath bushy eyebrows.

"I don't think we want to use the Toughs," he said slowly. "I said there are ten Masters, and that is correct. But they have a visitor who arrived by copter several days ago. A visitor and a prisoner."

"A prisoner?"

"Yes, a prisoner who wasn't sent down to the vats, but is kept on the upper floor. This prisoner is a black-haired, black-eyed woman."

"Maya!"

"Yes, I think the visitor is Nuwell Eli and the prisoner is your friend, Maya."

16

Nuwell Eli sat with Placer Viceroy, director of the Canfell Hydroponic Farm, in its large underground dining room, eating lunch. This meal was not the tasteless, gelatin-like food that was fed to the Jellies and Toughs and sold on the Martian market. It was a meal of thick, juicy steaks from the dome farms around Hesperidum and vegetables from the gardens inside the Mars City dome.

"We've been here better than a week, and she's still stubborn," Nuwell said morosely. "Surely she has the intelligence to realize how ridiculous and impractical is her sudden conversion to a lost rebel cause. I'm half convinced that this Kensington fellow put her under some sort of a hypnotic spell."

"You've been very gentle in your methods of conversion," said Placer. "It isn't like you, Nuwell. If you want quick results, we could turn her over to the Toughs for a while."

"No, I don't want her hurt. I love the woman and intend to marry her. The whippings and humiliations are as far as I'm willing to go."

"A peculiar sort of love, if you don't mind my saying so," remarked Placer.

Nuwell stared at him coldly.

"I do mind your saying so," he said. "My personal emotions are not subject to your interpretation. But Martian wives are expected to obey their husbands with deference and, by Saturn, I'm going to break her of that liberal terrestrial training!"

"You'd have the legal right to take the steps necessary for that, if she were married to you," Placer pointed out.

"But the little fool refuses to marry me now!" exclaimed Nuwell in exasperation. "If she hadn't refused, do you think I'd have brought her here? But I couldn't take her to one of the cities, except as a prisoner to be tried for sedition and treason, as long as she expresses this violent and open support of the rebel cause. Whether you consider it love or not, I want the woman for myself. I don't want her imprisoned or executed."

"Perhaps if she were presented with that alternative, she'd be more reasonable about it," murmured Placer.

"Don't you think I've threatened her with it? She just says that she'd rather die or go to prison than go back on her convictions and knuckle under to me. If she could only forget that she'd ever met that man Kensington!"

"Well, as for that, it might not be so hard to arrange," suggested Placer quietly.

Nuwell stared at him.

"What do you mean?" he asked.

"You're not familiar with the details of our work here, are you, Nuwell?"

"I thought I was, pretty well. But what you just said doesn't strike a chord."

"As you know, the Toughs and Jellies are originally criminals and vagabonds you have smuggled to us for experimental purposes. One major effect of our initial glandular experiments with them, which makes them into Toughs and Jellies, is that they lose all memory of their past."

"I don't want a flabby woman, like a Jelly!" exclaimed Nuwell with a shudder.

"I think we could eliminate the memory, permanently, without any physical changes at all," said Placer. "There are some pretty good scientists here. I expect the operation would cut down her thinking ability pretty heavily, though. I think it would still be slightly higher than that of the Jellies, but you couldn't ever expect her again to get above the intellectual level of a child of six or eight terrestrial years."

"I don't care anything about an intelligent woman," answered Nuwell ruthlessly. "If she weren't so proud of her intelligence now, I wouldn't have so much trouble with her. I want her as a beautiful woman, which is all a woman has a right to expect from a man, and if she were less intelligent and more tractable I might be able to train her to become the sort of wife a man of my profession and position requires."

Placer speared a bite of steak, casually, with his fork.

"Any time you say the word," he said carelessly.

"I'll give her the rest of today," said Nuwell with decision. "I'll work her over again with the whip this afternoon, and if she doesn't break I'll tell her what she can expect. Then, if that doesn't do the trick, I'll turn her over to you the first thing tomorrow."

"Tonight would be better," suggested Placer. "The initial surgery takes only about thirty minutes, and she'd do better to rest a night after that. It alone will remove a great deal of her volitional power. The entire series of operations will require about three days."

"Tonight it is, then," said Nuwell, "if she doesn't break this afternoon."

Maya sat in her locked room, her tunic and trousers covering the red welts on her back and legs. The tasteless gelatin which had been her only food since their arrival almost gagged her with every spoonful, but she had eaten all her lunch. She needed all the strength she could get to maintain her defiance.

She was in the grip of dull, unrelenting pain, physically and emotionally. Her flesh ached from yesterday's beating, and she was sick at heart at the revelation of Nuwell's essential brutality and callousness. She had thought him a sensitive and intelligent man, and she had admired him for this even after some of his exhibitions of childish temper had disillusioned her as to the glowing nobility which she had at first attributed to him.

She had felt a warm attraction to him and, when she thought Dark was dead, she had been willing to marry him on the basis, not of the passionate love she now felt for Dark, but of a mellow tenderness which she conceived a sound basis for an understanding life together.

But now! She shuddered at the thought that she might have married him, and perhaps lived all her life with him, thinking him to be gentle and kind. Whatever happened to her, she felt fortunate that this crisis had brought to her view the hidden side of him, that heretofore had been seen only by his partners in political manipulation and by the unfortunate victims of his prosecution.

Her shoulders drooped wearily. She stared across the room. It was as bare as a prison cell, which intrinsically it was.

There was a glass on the washbasin. It was made of heavy metal, with no sharp edges. Did Nuwell think she would commit suicide? Not as long as she knew Dark was alive!

Her mind touched the glass. It quivered. It tilted and fell to the floor with a clang.

She looked at it with mild curiosity as it rolled into a corner. She hadn't done that for a long time, not since she suppressed it because of Nuwell's hatred of witchcraft.

It was telekinesis. She had had the power since she was a child. It seemed that she remembered using it often, and in rather startling ways, when she was a small child with the Martians. But when she went to Earth, she gradually stopped playing with it, except in small ways when she was alone, because it seemed to make her elders very uncomfortable.

Telekinesis was ESP. It did not mean that she had any other ESP powers. But there was her experience in the copter....

Her mind reached out. At once, like a shock, she was in contact with Dark. His mind turned to hers at once.

Dark: *Maya! Where are you?*

Maya: *Come into my room, darling. I'm at the Canfell Hydroponic Farm. Are you still at Ultra Vires?*

Dark: *No, I'm in the vats below you. I knew you were here, but I didn't know where. I can see your room now, though, and its place in the building.*

Maya: *Can you free me?*

Dark: *Not now. There are four Toughs outside your door, guarding it. I can't attack them without arousing the Masters. Soon, though.*

Maya: *I don't know how I'm doing this. I didn't know I had telepathic powers.*

Dark: *A good many people have them, potentially. They don't have to have been "changed," as I was. But they usually require development.*

Maya: *I'm just glad I can, to know that you're here.*

Dark: *Maya, why are you in pain?*

Maya: *Nuwell has been whipping me, to try to get me to recant on my expressions of support for the rebel cause.*

There was a white-hot explosion in her brain that almost literally seared her mind. Staggered at its impact, she recognized it as the explosion of Dark's sudden anger. Then she was no longer in contact with him.

A hundred feet away, in another room, Nuwell pulled on a pair of black gloves and picked up a short, thick-lashed whip. Coiling the whip, he stepped out into the corridor, and turned toward Maya's room.

He met Placer, walking in the opposite direction.

"You're going to make your last try, now?" asked Placer.

"Yes," replied Nuwell. "I hope it works. Actually, her spirit and quick wit are among the reasons I like the girl. But I don't intend to be defied in this."

He proceeded on down the hall.

As he started past the barred gate to one of the ramps leading down into the vats below, the buzzer beside it sounded. A Jelly was standing behind the gate, fat, pathetic face pressed against the bars.

Nuwell stopped. No one else was in sight in the corridor.

"What do you want?" he asked the Jelly.

"Master, I seek entry in answer to the summons," replied the Jelly in a voice that quavered with fright.

"What summons?"

"It was ordered that one of us come above and do a task for the Masters," replied the Jelly. "I am one of those who must work today, and I have come in answer to the summons."

Nuwell looked up and down the corridor. He saw no one.

"What sort of task?" he asked, reluctant to accept the responsibility of admitting the Jelly.

"I don't know, Master."

"Look," said Nuwell, "I'm not a Master. I don't know anything about the summons. Someone else will have to let you in."

"If I'm late, they'll let the Toughs whip me!" wailed the Jelly pathetically. "Please let me in, Master!"

Nuwell, the whip coiled in his hand, impatient to get to Maya's room, was moved to pity at the creature's plight. Besides, the Jellies were harmless, and this one certainly wouldn't be seeking admittance without having been called.

"All right, then," said Nuwell, and flipped the switch.

The bars grated open and the Jelly came into the corridor. But as Nuwell reached out to activate the switch and close the gate, the Jelly, with surprising agility, slipped between him and the switch.

"What in space?" growled Nuwell. "Get out of the way!"

The Jelly did not move.

"I said get out of the way!" snapped Nuwell, shaking out the whip.

The Jelly cringed and its eyes were terrified, but it still stood against the switch, its huge, translucent body barring Nuwell.

"No, Master," it whimpered. "Don't shut the gate!"

Viciously, Nuwell slashed the whip across its naked shoulders, and the Jelly squealed with pain. Nuwell raised the whip again.

But then through the open gate there poured a solid mass of translucent flesh, a horde of naked Jellies. Silently, they tumbled into the corridor, filling it from wall to wall, and others behind them pushed to enter as they paused.

Wide-eyed, Nuwell stared at them for the briefest of moments. Then he dropped the whip and fled back up the hall, shouting at the top of his voice.

The door at the end of the corridor opened as Nuwell neared it, and Placer appeared in it. He held up a restraining hand.

"Don't make so much noise!" he snapped. "There's a conference going on in there. What's the—"

Voiceless now, Nuwell grasped Placer's arm and pointed, trembling, back down the corridor.

"What in space?" demanded Placer irritably, peering at the mass of Jellies pouring out of the gate and beginning to move hesitantly along the corridor in both directions.

"Jellies!" croaked Nuwell. "The Jellies are loose! They're attacking us!"

"Soft hunks of blubber!" said Placer contemptuously. "They can't hurt anybody. I wonder what idiot left that gate open?"

"I did," admitted Nuwell. "I mean, one of them wanted in and I let him in, and then he backed up against the switch so I couldn't close it, until the others came in."

"I don't know what sort of harebrained idea has gotten into their feeble minds," said Placer. "But I can take care of it in short order."

He stepped back into the room, and Nuwell heard him apologizing to the others for the disturbance. Then Placer reappeared, two whips in his hand, and closed the door behind him. He handed one of the whips to Nuwell.

"They're a lot more tractable than that woman of yours," said Placer. "Let's go."

Placer moved down the corridor toward the slowly advancing Jellies, and Nuwell followed reluctantly, at a respectable distance.

"Get back below!" shouted Placer at the Jellies as he neared them. "You know better than to come up here without permission!"

They stopped and milled as he approached them relentlessly, those in front trying to hold back and those behind them pushing them on. Placer moved straight up to them and began slashing right and left with his whip.

There was a sudden surge forward of the Jellies and Placer was engulfed. He vanished in a mass of seething, translucent flesh. Nuwell stopped, appalled, and began to edge backward.

There was a flurry of movement in the forefront of the Jellies, and Placer burst out of the group, his hair awry, his clothing torn, his whip gone. He staggered toward Nuwell at a half run.

"Get back to the room!" cried Placer. "I don't know what's stirred them up, but they can't be frightened back with whips!"

The two men ran back down the corridor and burst through the door, startling a conference group of five of the other Masters.

"Heatguns!" snapped Placer. "Something's stirred the Jellies up, and they're up here causing trouble! I'll turn the Toughs loose on them."

While two of the others hurried out another door for weapons and a third bolted the door through which the two men had just come, Placer picked up a microphone and switched on the amplifier system that covered every area of all levels of the Canfell Hydroponic Farm.

Into the microphone, he gave an animal call, a cry that started out on a low crooning note and rose in volume and intensity until it hurt the ears. He repeated this three times. Then he set the microphone down and turned back to his colleagues, an expression of satisfaction on his face.

"That releases the Toughs," he said. "Every Tough in the place is free to maim or kill any Jelly he sees, without fear of restraint or punishment. That should bring them to heel pretty quickly!"

17

Behind the locked door of the conference room, one of the Masters passed out heatguns to Nuwell, Placer and the other four.

"If we use these on them at half intensity, I think we can calm them down without killing any of them," said Placer. "We'll probably have more trouble beating down the Toughs and keeping them from killing all the Jellies than we will subduing the Jellies in the first place."

"I hope we warned the three at the other end of the hall in time," said one of the others. "There hasn't been any word from them."

Placer flicked a switch on the intercom system.

"Touchstone, are you men safe?" he asked.

"Yes, sir," replied a voice on the other end. "We locked ourselves in, because there aren't any heatguns we can get to from here. The Jellies haven't gotten this far down yet. They seem to be cowed by the Toughs at the door to Miss Cara Nome's room, and the Toughs are strutting around getting themselves in the mood for an attack. We've been watching them through the window."

"Good," said Placer. "Between the Toughs at that end and our heatguns at this end, we ought to be able to force them back below without much trouble. Are we ready to move out?"

A different voice came in over the intercom, the voice of the tenth Master, who was on duty in the farm's control room.

"Placer, the screens show three groundcars moving up from the south," he said. "I've tried to contact them by radio, but they don't answer."

"We haven't been notified to expect any government visitors," said Placer. "It may be a convoy of travelers off-course in the desert, or it could be a wandering party of escaped rebels. Warn them away."

"Yes, sir."

Touchstone's voice came in from the other end of the hall.

"The Toughs are attacking, Placer. Space, it's awful! Those poor Jellies can't stand up to the Toughs."

Suddenly his voice changed, and became shrill with excitement.

"Placer! One of those Jellies has a heatgun! Two of the Toughs were just burned down, and the others are falling back down the hall. The Jellies are coming on, and I can see the gun in the hand of one of them."

"Great space!" muttered Placer. "All right, Touchstone. Hold tight and keep that door locked. We'll get to you."

He turned to the others.

"We've got to move out now," he said. "Use full intensity and shoot to kill. We'll have to burn our way through those Jellies and get to the other end of the hall."

Leaving one of the Masters at the intercom in the control room, the other six went out into the corridor, heatguns ready. The foremost Jellies had advanced almost to the door, and now that they had spread out along the corridor, they were not packed so closely together.

The six men advanced steadily, leveling their guns. They fired, intense, almost invisible beams stabbing into the group of Jellies.

Jellies shrieked in pain, several of them collapsing to the floor with smoking flesh. The others turned in panic and began to crowd back down the corridor, the beams stabbing at them and picking them off one by one.

Then, from amid the Jellies, a beam struck forth, and one of the Masters went down, his face burned away.

Placer burned down the Jelly holding the heatgun, and the five survivors moved grimly on.

On the ramp ahead, Dark and Old Beard approached the open gate to the corridor, Happy and Shadow following them.

"I wish I had been able to find more heatguns at Ultra Vires," said Dark to Old Beard. "Only three, besides our four, are spreading them out pretty thin."

"At least the Jellies made the break into the corridor, and we've managed to discourage the Toughs below from following them up for a while," said Old Beard. The bodies of a dozen Toughs at the foot of the ramp behind them attested to the rear guard battle they had fought. That was what had held them up so long. "If we can hold the corridor and keep the Masters bottled up, your friends outside should be able to turn the tide."

"It will take them a while to break in," said Dark. "But I've already contacted Cheng telepathically and told him to move in."

They emerged into the corridor, into a scene of tremendous confusion. All they could see in both directions were Jellies, milling about and chattering. The mass seemed to be drifting gradually toward the left, while from the right came shrieks of agony.

"This way," said Dark, turning to the left. "We have to get Maya out of here before we can do anything else."

Forcing their way through the Jellies, they came to a door. Dark tried it. It was locked. He burned the lock off and pushed it open.

Maya was standing back against the wall on the other side of the room, alarmed at the noise in the corridor, frightened at the opening of the door. As Dark and Old Beard came in, and she recognized Dark, she ran across the room to meet them, joy transforming her face.

She threw herself into Dark's arms.

"Oh, Dark!" she cried. "I knew you'd come!"

He enfolded her in his arms and kissed her. Then he turned back to Old Beard, his arm around Maya's shoulders.

"Old Beard, this is Maya Cara Nome," said Dark. "Maya, this is my father, the real Dark Kensington."

"The older Dark Kensington," corrected Old Beard. "I am very happy to meet you, Maya. My son, you have chosen a beautiful woman."

Happy and Shadow had followed the other two into the room and were standing against the door, holding it closed.

"Maya, we're going to have to try to hold the corridor until the Phoenix gets here," said Dark. "I want you to go with Shadow and Happy down to the vats. You get into a marsuit, and they'll take you to one of the entrance buildings. I'll tell Cheng to pick you up in one of the groundcars, and then Happy and Shadow can come back here to help us."

"I'll do nothing of the sort," said Maya flatly. "You need them up here now, and I won't leave you. I'm going to stay here and help you. After all, I can handle a heatgun better than any of these Jellies."

"But, Maya, I want to know that you're safe."

"I don't want to be safe until you are. Please let me stay, Dark."

"All right," Dark surrendered. "Shadow, give her your heatgun."

The five of them left the room together.

They emerged into a scene of incredible carnage. The Jellies, with only three heatguns which they were inept at using, had been no match for the Masters. Almost all of the Jellies were lying dead on the floor of the corridor, and the remaining few were backed up at the end of the hall to their right.

Three of the men were advancing toward these last Jellies. The other two, returning to the conference room, already had passed Maya's door and were picking their way back among the scorched, twitching bodies of the

Jellies. Dark and the others were between these two retreating forces of Masters.

"We'll have to try to save those Jellies," decided Dark at once. "Happy, you and Shadow move back up the corridor and hold the line in case those other two turn back to attack our rear. The rest of us will tackle the three to the right."

They split up and moved off. But they were too late. Dark, Maya and Old Beard had advanced hastily no more than ten feet when the last of the Jellies at the end of the corridor collapsed under the combined beams of three heatguns. Immediately, the door beyond the dead Jellies opened and three more Masters emerged. They joined the first three, and were given the heatguns taken from the vanquished Jellies.

Dark stopped and held up his hand, halting the advance of his little group.

"We're too badly outnumbered now," he said. "Let's collect Happy and Shadow and get back down to the vats, where we can hide until the Phoenix break in."

The Masters had seen them now, and started to move up the corridor toward them in a group, but were still ten or fifteen feet out of heatgun range. Dark was not surprised to see that one of the group was Nuwell.

Dark and Maya turned back toward the entrance toward the underground vats, but stopped as Old Beard emitted a growl of recognition.

One of the three men who had emerged from the room was skinny, goateed Goat Hennessey, and he was coming forward now in the forefront of the group, a heatgun in his hand.

"Dark, you and Maya go on without me," said Old Beard very quietly. "I have a score to settle."

Dark turned back, his mouth open to protest, but Old Beard had already started swiftly down the corridor toward the oncoming group.

"Wait!" cried Dark, and started to run after him. But, in his haste, Dark tripped over the corpse of a Jelly and fell sprawling. In the moments it took Dark to scramble to his feet and recover his dropped heatgun from the floor, the drama ahead of him flashed like lightning to its conclusion.

Old Beard ran down the corridor toward the group of Masters, leaping lightly over the bodies of Jellies in his path, his gray hair streaming out behind him.

"Goat Hennessey!" he thundered, his voice reverberating from the walls of the corridor. "You betrayed me and killed my wife! Now the time has come for you to pay for your crimes!"

The Masters stopped in their tracks, frozen at the sight of this figure of retribution charging down on them. In their forefront, Goat stood staring, open-mouthed, not comprehending until the full impact of Old Beard's words broke upon him. Then, recognition dawning, he squawled in amazement and fear:

"Dark Kensington!"

With that cry, Goat turned in terror to escape. But Dark was now within range, and the intense beam of his downward-chopping heatgun caught Goat at the base of the skull and swept all the way down his back. Goat Hennessey plunged forward to the floor, dead, his spine burned away.

Even as Goat fell, his companions emerged from their paralysis. The beams of five heatguns focussed on Old Beard, and he died in a burst of flame that flared from wall to wall of the narrow corridor.

Appalled at his father's sudden death, Dark almost leaped after him, to attack the five survivors single-handed. But Maya grasped his arm.

"No, Dark!" she urged. "Please don't!"

Realizing on the instant that to die now would only leave Maya at the mercy of the Masters and Nuwell, Dark turned back. He and Maya ran for the door to the ramp leading underground, Dark calling to Happy and Shadow to join them.

But Happy, and presumably the invisible Shadow, were well up the corridor and they, too, were under attack now. The two Masters who had been heading for the conference room had turned back and were now in range of Happy, their heatguns blasting.

Happy had remained true to Dark's charge to hold the line against any attack from the rear. Frightened but staunch, he was standing his ground, waving his own heat beam at the approaching pair of Masters.

But Happy was too unfamiliar with the weapon and too nervous to hit either of his targets. The beams of both Masters found him at the same time, and, with a woeful shriek that was cut off in a choking gurgle, the unfortunate Jelly collapsed to a smoking heap on the floor, quivered once and lay still.

Apparently from out of nowhere, the unarmed Shadow descended like a thunderbolt on one of Happy's killers. The surprised Master went sprawling, his heatgun flying from his hand.

Shadow might have vanquished the other, too, except that this startled individual, waving his heat beam wildly in an attempt to catch the elusive, vanishing and reappearing figure, scored a lucky hit. There was a tremendous flare of flame, and the extraordinary form of Shadow appeared for the last time, a charred, flat body lying on the floor of the corridor like the shadow for which he had been named.

The whole tragedy ran its course in less than a minute. In that time, Dark and Maya reached the entrance to the ramp, ducked into it and ran down the incline to the sheltering dimness of the labyrinthine vats.

18

Moments later, the two groups of Masters converged at the gate, two from one direction and five from the other.

"After them!" commanded Placer. "But stay together. We'll have to try to hunt them down in the vats, and maybe the Toughs can help us, but we don't want to get separated so they can pick us off one by one."

"Wait, Placer, there's something you ought to know," said one of the two Masters who had come from the direction of the conference room. "Greyde called out a few minutes ago to tell us he had word from Vidonati in the control room. Those groundcars that were hanging around had attacked one of the entrance buildings."

"Space!" growled Placer. "There must be a conspiracy involved here somewhere. We'd better stay up here, then."

He pulled the lever beside the gate to the ramp, and it rumbled down and crashed into place.

"At least, those two are trapped below," he said with satisfaction. "We can hunt them down at our leisure when we've repelled this attack from outside. If we can take them alive, I'm of a mind to make them pay well for their responsibility in our losing all our experimental Jellies."

The seven of them went on to the conference room, picking their way among the bodies of the Jellies. Placer took over the intercom from Greyde.

"Vidonati, this is Placer," he said. "What's the situation?"

"The groundcars attacked the south building," replied Vidonati. "They moved in and concentrated all three car beams on the airlock and burned it through. I counted nine men in marsuits who left the groundcars and went into the building. Of course, as soon as they started blasting the airlocks, I closed the emergency barrier to block off the downward ramp."

"Obviously, since we still have air in the place," commented Placer dryly. "You'd better call Mars City and get them to send help."

"I've already done that," said Vidonati. "A jet squadron's on its way."

"Good," said Placer. "They can be here in about five hours, and it will take those rebels, or whoever they are, two or three times that long to burn through one of the emergency barriers, even if they blast an opening and bring their groundcars into the building to bring the groundcars' big guns on it."

"Should I stick it out here, or seal all the barriers and come below?" asked Vidonati. The control room was in the north building.

"Stay up there so you can report on what they're doing, unless they start to move toward that building," instructed Placer. "If they do, seal the other emergency barriers at once and come below. We can switch to the emergency radio down here to keep in touch with the task force from Mars City, and just wait it out underground until they clean up these rebels."

"Good enough," agreed Vidonati. "I won't take any chances."

In the vats below, Dark and Maya made their way to Old Beard's hideout, their heatguns ready, keeping a sharp lookout for Toughs. They reached it without incident.

Dark looked sadly around the little recess beneath the tangled vegetation, where Old Beard had concealed himself successfully so long from both Toughs and Masters. He had hoped that this reunion with his father would mean many years of companionship between them, once they were free of the Canfell Hydroponic Farm and had found a haven in the Icaria Desert.

But he knew that Old Beard had died in an act that had great meaning to him, a savage revenge that had wiped out the bitter memory of the loss of his wife and had repaid him for twenty-five long years of exile. Old Beard had died nobly.

Dark picked up one of the smaller marsuits.

"We don't know what's going to happen above, and we can't help much by staying inside, now that we can't hold that corridor and bottle them up in a room until Cheng and the Phoenix break in," said Dark. "We'd best get up to one of the exit buildings, get out through the airlock and get picked up by one of the groundcars. I don't need a marsuit, but you can put that on as soon as we get above in the building."

"Have you been in telepathic touch with Cheng?" asked Maya.

"Yes. They've already broken into the south building. That's the one I came through when I left for Ultra Vires and when I came back. But the Masters let down a heavy emergency barrier on the ramp when they attacked the airlock, and we wouldn't be able to get through that. There's a ramp near here that Old Beard told me opens onto the north building. We'll go there, and I'll send a call to Cheng to move over and meet us there."

Dark sent out a call to Cheng and received an acknowledgement. He and Maya started for the ramp, unaware that the building which was their goal housed the farm's control room, and the watching Vidonati.

Above, a few moments later, Vidonati called Placer on the intercom.

"Placer, they've come back to the groundcars and turned them in this direction," said Vidonati. "I'm going to let down the barriers on the ramps from the east and west buildings, sabotage the controls so they can't raise them again, and come on down. I'll lower the barrier to this building from inside, as soon as I get past it on the ramp."

"All right," said Placer. "We'll start getting the emergency radio in operation down here. Do a good job, but do it fast, and don't get caught up there by the rebels blasting the airlock."

"I won't," promised Vidonati. "It'll only take me a few minutes, and I can be down the ramp before they can focus their beams on the airlock."

In the lead groundcar, as the three of them wheeled around and headed slowly for the north building, Cheng turned to one of his companions with a frown.

"I've been trying to get through telepathically to Dark, but I can't reach him," said Cheng. "He didn't give any instructions for getting into the building, but they seem to have locked these airlocks by remote control so they can't be operated. We'll have to blast this one as we did the other one, because I don't imagine Dark will be able to open it from inside. He seemed in rather a hurry to be picked up."

Dark and Maya hurried up the ramp toward the north building. Dark had been concentrating too heavily on finding his way through the vats to receive Cheng's telepathic call.

They passed the barred gate that opened into the corridors of the upper level, and a few moments later reached the top of the ramp and the gate to the north building. Dark had been prepared to open this by telekinesis but, to his surprise, it was already open.

They passed through it and emerged into the north building.

Dark had never seen one of the ground-level buildings in daylight, as both times he had passed through the south building it had been night. He looked around the place curiously as they entered.

It was about fifty feet square, bare except for the low, hard bunks on which the Toughs slept at night. On three sides of it were windows, now closed with heavy steel shutters. The airlock was across the room, opposite the ramp entrance. The fourth wall was blank, and apparently shut off a room at the end, because there was a closed door in the center of it.

They moved out into the room, and Dark said:

"Slip into your marsuit, and we'll go out the airlock. I told Cheng to bring the groundcars over this way, and they ought to be ready to pick us up by the time we get out."

"I don't see why we didn't stay down in the vats until the Phoenix break in," said Maya. "We were well hidden down there, and there might have been some way we could have helped the Phoenix from inside."

"Primarily because I'm not sure now that the Phoenix can break in," answered Dark. "I didn't know about that heavy emergency barrier the Masters let down on the south ramp, and I was surprised and relieved to find they hadn't dropped one on this ramp, too. If they had, we'd have been trapped below. If they have those barriers on all four ramps, the Phoenix can't stay around long enough to burn through them, because the Masters have probably already called for help from Mars City."

Maya had laid her marshelmet down on one of the bunks, and was pulling the marsuit on over her tunic and trousers.

The door at the other end of the room opened, and a man emerged, a heatgun in his hand.

Vidonati stopped in his tracks, startled, at the sight of Dark and Maya. Dark grunted in surprise, and reached for his heatgun.

Even as Dark freed his weapon, Vidonati fired. The beam missed them, melting away the top of Maya's marshelmet and setting the bunk aflame. Then, as the beam of Dark's gun swung toward him, Vidonati ducked precipitately back into the control room.

"He got your marshelmet!" exclaimed Dark. "We're going to have to go in and flush him out of there, and just hope there's another marsuit in there, before we can open the airlock."

Heatgun in hand, Dark started for the door of the control room, Maya at his heels.

It was then that the Phoenix, the three groundcars drawn up with their heavy guns focused, blasted the airlock of the north building. In seconds, the airlock was burned through.

There was no emergency barrier down on this ramp. The heavy, Earth-pressured air of the north building whistled out into the desert. As from a punctured balloon, the pressured atmosphere of the entire Canfell Hydroponic Farm rushed after it, roaring up the ramp, in a moment stripping the vats, the upper level and the north building.

Caught in the tornadic blast, Dark could only cling to a bolted-down cot with one hand, and hold onto Maya around the waist with the other. As the pressure dropped precipitately and oxygen no longer touched his lungs, he could actually feel his alternate metabolism shifting into gear, he could feel his breathing stop and the glow of solar energy begin to spread through his body.

As the wind faded and died, Dark released Maya and rose exultantly to his feet. Down below, he knew, Nuwell and the Masters were gasping out their lives in the thin air, like beached fish. Their recent attacker, Vidonati, lay half out of the door of the control room, his hands clutching convulsively at the floor.

"That's not the way I'd planned it, but it's just as good!" Dark exclaimed. "We've taken the farm!"

Then he remembered. Maya had no marshelmet!

Appalled, struck to the heart, he turned in his tracks.

Maya was standing behind him, calmly trying to rearrange her raven hair, tangled by the raging rush of wind.

"What's the matter?" she asked quietly, becoming aware of Dark's intent gaze.

"Maya! You don't have a helmet on! Are you breathing?"

She was silent for a moment, apparently examining herself.

"Why, no, I don't believe I am," she replied, just as calmly.

"How can you ...? Wait a minute!"

Dark sent his mind into the invisible. His probing thoughts fled over desert and lowland, seeking. They found the Martian, Qril, and he recognized that Qril responded immediately.

Qril, how is it that Maya is able to live in the Martian atmosphere without breathing? asked Dark telepathically.

She is as you, replied Qril. *When she was a child, living among the Martians, we altered her physiological and genetic structure so that she, also, is able to utilize solar energy and exist without oxygen.*

Why didn't you tell me this before, at Ultra Vires? demanded Dark.

You did not ask, replied Qril, and the mental contact faded out.

Dark turned to Maya, his face alight.

"Darling," he said, "our children will need no embryonic alterations. They will be born as we are, able to live under Martian conditions. And never again will either of us ever have to wear a marsuit!"

He felt the questing touch of Cheng's mind.

Cheng: *Are you there, Dark?*

Dark: *Here.*

Cheng: *Are you all right?*

Dark: *We're both fine! We're coming out. Then we'll take off at once for the Icaria Desert, before the Mars City task force gets here.*

He and Maya walked hand in hand through the blasted airlock. The three groundcars were there, waiting.

The two of them stood for a moment, before getting aboard the groundcars, and looked out together across the red desert toward the sinking sun.

Death? Desolation? No, not for them. This was life, and free, bleak beauty, for them and for their children. The future of Mars was theirs.

And Now a Message . . .
By Greg Fowlkes

A short Story from the upcoming Book - *Back Road to the Stars*

And Now A Message...

For the third time that night Jack Olsen was about to nod off over the copy of *Statistical Information Theory* that he was attempting to read. Giving it up as a bad effort, he shut the book and looked out the window of the control room at the giant bowl of the Arecibo radio telescope. Theoretically he was running the huge instrument, but in reality all the controlling was being done by the computers in the room around him. For six months he had been working eight hour shifts every night, and his job had consisted of the five minutes a shift that it took to enter the coordinates to be examined on the control console. Other than that, he was on hand only for the off chance that the monitoring programs would recognize some pattern in the radio noise, in which case an alarm would sound. So far, in the six months, it hadn't happened.

He walked over to the coffee machine in the hopes that a cup would revive him enough so that he could continue his studies. He never made it, for as if to prove the lie of his earlier thoughts, the alarm sounded. For a moment Jack was frozen, the alarm beating raucously in his ears, then he pulled himself together and flicked off the switch on the bell. With the room returned to the relative quiet of the whoosh of the cooling fans on the equipment, Jack sat down at the console and keyed in an enquiry. Within seconds the computer had replied that it was receiving a strong periodic signal on the 42 centimeter band. Further questioning showed that it was not a program malfunction but a genuine signal.

Jack picked up the phone and dialed his boss's number. It was three in the morning, but his instructions had been clear. If anything was received that could possibly be an intelligent signal, he was supposed to contact his superior immediately.

Despite the long drive through the mountains in the cool Puerto Rican night, Professor Kraft showed up with his eyes still sleepy. Shuffling over to the coffee pot by the window he poured himself a large mug before he said anything. "You'd better have something good to get me up at this hour."

"I think so," Jack said, aware that his boss's irritation was only feigned. "I've been checking with the computer since I called you. It shows a strong periodic signal with a sharp pulse every fifty milliseconds. It runs on like that for about two and a half minutes before the signal fades below the background."

"Any chance that it might be a pulsar?" Kraft asked, referring to the radio signals of rapidly rotating neutron stars. "That's within the range of periods for them. When the first one was discovered, they thought that they had received intelligent signals."

"I thought of that, so I checked the record of the broad band receiver." Jack brought out a long strip of graph paper and pointed to the evenly spaced patterns of peaks on it. "Where the narrow band shows only a single repetitive pulse, the wide band gives us this fine structure. It's far too regular to be a pulsar and much too detailed. It's more like some sort of timing signal or spacer. And in between the pulses there is another signal. It's not as repetitive as the main pulse. That's why the program doesn't bring it out. But there definitely is some sort of transmission in between. It's weaker, but I think that we can write a processing program to pick it out from the noise."

Kraft looked at the trace in his hand thoughtfully. "I hate to make snap judgements. You can be suckered in too easily that way. But it does look like some kind of artificial signal. We'll get the team working on it in the morning. Have you received any additional signals?"

"No. I've kept the dish tracking the source, but all we get on 42 cm. is background noise. It's like there was a moment of freak atmospheric conditions that opened a window, and then it shut again. Just like you get with shortwave sometimes because of the ionosphere."

"Well, we should be grateful for what we've got. I don't think I can sleep anymore tonight, so I'll keep you company. I'd like to be here if we get any more messages from our friends out there," he said, pointing with his cup towards the star filled sky that loomed over the radio telescope's antenna.

"Frustrating, isn't it?" Prof. Kraft remarked to the team of graduate students and post doctoral fellows that were working under him on the interstellar communications project. And frustrating it had been. For six months they had continuously monitored the sky searching for signs of life finally to be rewarded by a two minute snippet of extraterrestrial conversation.

Now, another six months later, they had still made no sense of the signal, nor had they received any further transmissions from that part of the sky, though they had concentrated their efforts in that direction.

"Rumors have leaked out about our discovery, and I've been getting requests for the data. I'd sure hate to have someone else steal our thunder by deciphering the signal, but if we don't make some progress soon, we're going to have to release it." He looked around the table at the young faces of his assistants. At the moment they didn't look nearly as bright and intelligent as he knew they were.

"Why don't I summarize what we've found so far in hopes that it will give us some new ideas?"

"First, we've got this repetitive pattern of pulses every twentieth of a second as regular as clockwork. So regular, in fact, that we can't decide whether they serve as breaks in the message or were just put there to attract our attention. Remember, it was these pulses that were first recognized by the computer."

"But the pulses aren't the real message. That lays in the spaces in between. We've been able to deduce that the messages are digitized and the computer has been able to enhance them so that we have a fairly error free record of them. There is some repetitive structure to them, and they do vary in some sort of progression, but beyond that, we haven't been able to get the least notion of what they mean. Anyone have something to add?"

Bill Warden, one of the post docs, spoke up. "Well, we've tried mathematical analysis on the signals and have gotten zero results. It has already been assumed that any sort of interstellar communications would be based on sort of easily recognizable mathematical progression. Like one, two three. Something like that to show that they were rational. From there you can always build up more complicated concepts."

"With this message we don't have that, which leads us to one of two assumptions. One, we have only a fragment of a broadcast, and from a very advanced lesson at that. If that's the case, I don't see much hope of our being able to decipher the message until we can receive more signals to give us a broader base to work from."

"The other alternative is that they, whoever they are, just don't think like us. Their minds work in some fashion so that this mess we have makes sense to them. If so, I don't see any hope at all. Their minds may just be too foreign for us to hold a dialog with them."

"Thank you for that optimistic note," Prof. Kraft said wryly. "For the first time mankind has received a message from another species and we can't tell whether it is a cure for cancer, a means of achieving universal peace, or a recipe for sauerbratten. Any comments?"

"If it's sauerbratten, where do we go for a tablespoon of powdered bandersnatch egg?" quipped one of the grad students. They all laughed at the joke more than it deserved. Six months of unrewarded work had left them all a little giddy. After the giggles and comments had died down, Jack Olsen coughed, trying to get their attention.

"You've got something useful to say, Jack?" Kraft asked. "You might as well tell us. I don't think anyone else has anything useful to add," he said, pointedly looking at the wisecracker.

"I've been thinking about the signal, and I remember something that I said to you the night it came in. I don't know if you recall, but I called the pulses timing signals. Now there is one type of common transmission that has the same kind of pulses, and that's television. They use the pulses to synchronize the frames. It's possible that the message in between each pulse is a picture, and the whole transmission is meant to be viewed in sequence."

"How long have you been sitting on this while the rest of us were beating our brains out?" Kraft asked.

"It just came to me," Jack said, his face flushed. "I should have thought of it earlier, but like Bill said, we've all been conditioned to look for something like one plus one equals two."

"I think that we should all have seen it," Kraft said. "It makes as much sense as anything else that's been suggested. Do you think that you can get us a picture?"

"If it's there, I should be able to pick it out using the computer," Jack answered.

"Good. Then, since it was your idea, you're in charge. Dragoon anything or anybody that you need to help you."

Five days later they were all gathered around the conference room table again, but this time there was a TV set and a video recorder on a cart at its end. From the nervous stubbing of cigarette butts and fingers drumming on the table, it was obvious that all the members of the team were in a state of anticipation.

"It took some time to figure out exactly how the signal was put together," Jack began. "After all, we didn't know how many lines there were in each frame or how many bits made up each unit of picture. In the end, I had to have the computer run through all the likely possibilities for one of the frames. It took a lot of computer time, but I've finally got some recognizable pictures."

"It turns out that the original broadcast was in color. That threw us for a while, but we finally psyched it out. The aliens must have eyes structurally different from ours; there are only two colors, not three in the signal. Which colors they are is anybody's guess. They might be ultraviolet and infrared for all we can tell. Arbitrarily, I've assigned them red and bluish green, so keep that in mind. Also, because the video recorder uses thirty frames a second instead of the twenty in the transmission, it was necessary to compress the program a bit. This means that everything you'll be seeing has been speeded up about fifty percent.

"I guess you're all more interested in seeing the tape than in listening to me." A snort from Prof. Kraft indicated agreement. Jack flicked off the lights and started the tape. For a minute the screen showed only snow, then a face became recognizable. It was a sickly chartreuse, and there was no nose between the two large, oval eyes, but it was recognizable as a face. The figures movements were quick and jerky like an old silent movie, the result of the difference in frame speed, and the picture left a lot to be desired in clarity, the product of interstellar noise, but it was a picture, the first of an alien race.

As the tape played, a weird, sings song voice came from the speaker sounding something like a Chinese chipmunk. "I forgot to mention that there was also an audio track along with the signal. Again, it's only a reconstruction and may not bear much resemblance to the original, but then, we'll never know," Jack commented. They had determined that the source of the transmission was at least several dozen light years away. It would take twice that number of years to send a message and receive a reply, by which time they would all be dead.

They continued to watch the tape. The camera had drawn back to show the alien from the waist up revealing rounded shoulders and a pair of six fingered hands. Apparently he was standing behind a low lectern or a table of some sort. The fuzzy picture and camera angle made it hard to tell which. As he, or her, or it, spoke, the alien pointed at a chart or poster suspended on the backdrop. A pattern of red and blue that hurt the eye with violent contrasts seemed to be some sort of text. The voice continued as the picture disappeared in a sea of snow and then it broke into static. The transmission had ended.

"You've done a fine job, Jack," Prof. Kraft said after they had played the tape through a half dozen times. "It's actually far better than I thought it would be, and I think we can accept any of the shortcomings that you mentioned."

"So, we've got a face and body of what certainly is a rational creature. He seemed to be giving us a lesson or lecture of some sort, though I for one don't have the faintest idea of what he was talking about. We have an idea of what they look like which I am sure will give the biologists a lot to speculate on, so I guess that we should be thankful for small favors, but I still don't see how we're going to learn any more about them without receiving further signals."

"I wouldn't hold out much hope of that," Jack interjected. "I think that it's clear now that the signal we picked up was not meant for interstellar communication. Any such signal would have been designed with much greater noise immunity. We were able to receive it only because of an accident of atmospheric conditions. It was actually just a local TV broadcast. As we haven't received anything since, those conditions must be rare."

"So," Kraft said, "we have a message of great potential import, that at the very least could provide us with insights on a totally alien culture, and no way to decipher it."

"I've got an idea," Bill said. "We've all been looking at the problem from the point of view of hardware and computer programs. That's natural because of our backgrounds, but now that we have what amounts to an artifact, maybe we should call in a specialist. We need someone who is trained in resurrecting a culture from its fragments. I suggest that we show the tape to some archeologists and get their opinions."

Convincing an archeologist to look at the tape was harder than it had sounded. Most of them were more interested in ancient rather than alien civilizations. Jack suspected that they felt out of their depth with the computers and electronics. With some pressure and pleading, a group finally agreed to view the tape, but after the showing, only one evinced any interest in following up on it.

A visiting lecturer from Norway, she was reputed to have a good background in languages, though Jack lacked the knowledge to judge her qualifications. However, as she was young, blond, and attractive, he was quite willing to spend the time required to familiarize her with the tape and the equipment they had used to come up with it. Together, they spent hours viewing the tape, studying it frame by frame attempting to pick out the slightest piece of information.

The project team had been assembled in the conference room, and this time it was the archeologist's turn to address them. For three weeks Cristina Peterson had been studying the tape almost constantly, and now she was ready to give her opinion. With the exception of Jack, who had been working closely with her, they were all, even Prof. Kraft, eagerly awaiting the report. There had been a great deal of speculation about what her findings would be.

"First," she began, "before I get your hopes up, I want to say that I have not been able to get a word for word translation of the voice on the tape. The sample of speech is just too brief for that to be possible. If the scene had contained more action, I might have been more successful, but we were not that fortunate. I have, however, been able to form a hypothesis based on the spoken word as well as visual clues such as facial expression, setting, and so on."

"An important point to remember is that the aliens, despite certain differences in appearance, are not too dissimilar from ourselves. They are bipedal, intelligent, and possess opposable thumbs. They have binocular vision and a form of color perception as well. Brain size is about the same in relationship to total body size as in humans, and I would be greatly surprised if they were much larger or smaller than ourselves. That much can be guessed on the basis of physiology from the picture and the nature of the signal. From this information, I think that we can draw the conclusion that their planet is, within limits, earthlike."

"Probably more relevant is their state of culture. They obviously have a technology and one that is recognizable in terms of our own. That we can receive their signals is proof of that. Also, they speak, they wear clothing, we can even guess at the purpose of some of the objects visible in the tape. I might add that this is more than we can do for some of the artifacts of primitive human cultures. In some ways we have more in common with the aliens than we do with the Tasadi or Bushman."

"I want you to bear in mind that these beings are not greatly different from ourselves. If we are to properly analyze the contents of the message, we must remember that they are influenced by the same drives and forces as humans." There was an uneasy shifting in their seats on the part of the team members as they took in the meaning of her statement.

"If we accept this premise, and replace the alien with a human, we can make an educated guess as to what we are seen on the tape. I'll run it again for you so that you can make the substitution." Jack tapped the switch, and for the next minute and a half they watched the now familiar scene replay itself.

"Before I give my own opinion, would anyone else like to make a guess?" Cristina asked.

Kraft looked around the room, but it appeared as though no one had the courage to be the first to put his own views forward. To break the silence he said, "It's only a guess, but to start the discussion, I'd say that the alien might be a lecturer. He's obviously standing at some sort of podium or speaker's table."

"He seems a little too impassioned for a lecturer, at least in the physical sciences," one of the grad students remarked. "I've never seen you that excited before a class." Kraft smiled at the reference to his own low keyed classroom delivery.

"Maybe it's a political science class. They get more aroused."

Bill Warden broke in, "Why a class? It looks to me more like he's a politician trying to persuade the voters. He must be up for reelection. The sign in back could be an election poster." That brought a couple of laughs and a few less than serious comments.

"We've all had a crack at it," Prof. Kraft said. "You obviously have your own interpretation, and I think that we've been kept in suspense long enough. From the look on Jack's face, it must be a good one. Let's hear it now. After all, the communication between two species is one of the most important events in human history."

She smiled at the jibe. "All your suggestions are plausible, but I've spent more time analyzing the tape than you have. I'll play it again for you and point out the features that have led me to my interpretation."

"The first thing that caught my attention was the fact that the word 'gratach' was mentioned fourteen times, an unusually high incidence in such a brief speech. Furthermore, at least four of those times the speaker pointed to the symbols on the chart behind him. I think that we can assume that 'gratach' is a name, and the symbols form the written version."

"Now here's something that I want you to see." She froze the picture on the television. "Note the artifacts on the table, a bowl filled with a substance and a box or container. There appears to be some writing on the box, but the resolution of the picture isn't good enough to allow us to make it out. However," she said as the tape began to roll again, "as the alien points to the box and says 'gratach' it is likely that the symbols again spell out the name in the chart behind the alien. Note, too, the expression on his face. Despite the lack of a nose, the face is surprisingly human, and if that expression was on a human face, it would be one of approval or pleasure."

"I think that if you put all the clues together, you can come to only one conclusion. Dr. Warden was not far off when he suggested a political campaign. The speaker is definitely trying to persuade his audience, but it is the package, not himself, that he is trying to sell."

"Oh, god," Kraft sputtered. "You can't mean it. The first communication from another planet and it's only . . ."

"Yes, I'm afraid so," Cristina said. "The first and only signal received from another world is nothing more than a breakfast food commercial."

Special Preview!

The Laws of Magic
By Greg Fowlkes
© 2010

Now available from The Fictional Press
www.TheFictionalPress.com

THE LAWS OF MAGIC
WITHOUT LICENSE

☆   ☆   ☆   ☆   ☆

As Egil Njalsson climbed the steps of the criminal courts building he wondered if it was really worth it. Eighteen months of practicing law on his own and here he was in his only suit, about to attend the preliminary hearing in a petty case for which with luck he would be able to recover his expenses. It wasn't even a paying client. The state would be picking up the tab for this one, and he'd ended up being the lawyer appointed by the court. At the moment it wasn't clear who would benefit most from the charity, the client or the lawyer. He hadn't had a case in three months and he'd just been eking out a living writing briefs for other lawyers. He could do that well enough. His technical background gave him a depth of knowledge most lawyers lacked when it came to cases involving points of science as well as law. If he hadn't had that he'd be starving.

He'd been thinking about that a lot lately; whether he had made the right decision giving up science and going into the law. At the time, with the aerospace industry in a depression in the early seventies, it had seemed like a good idea. Engineers were pumping gas and PhD's in physics were selling insurance. Being a lawyer had seemed like a good way to make money. A stable income, no ups and downs. He'd put in his time at law school and done well. After the grind at CalThaum, law school had been a snap. So here he was a lawyer barely making ends meet and his school mates, the ones who had stuck with science were all making it rich designing personal calculating engines and disk storage units.

He tried to put all these thoughts out of his mind as he passed through the big brass doors of the court house. After all, he did have a client to defend, and a duty to him. It wasn't easy, though. It wasn't, after all, a very important case. Just a charge of fortune telling and practicing the Art without a license. Minor offenses, probably not even any jail time involved. This wouldn't even be a trial today, just a plea and arranging of bail.

It wouldn't even have amounted to that if his client hadn't instisted on pleading not guilty. He'd met him at the county jail, an old man, one Jake Schmidts. He'd tried to talk him out of pleading not guilty, too. A guilty plea, a small fine, and they both could be done with it. His client, though, had turned out to be something of a character. So here he was.

It took an hour and a half before their case came up. The judge looked at him questioningly when he had pleaded not guilty, but thankfully had released his client on his own recognizance when he indicated he had a permanent address. It was over in five minutes.

They got the release papers and the court date from the bailiff. Egil started to head out when he noticed that his client seemed lost and disoriented by it all. "Do you have car fare home?"

"No," Schmidts said. "I didn't have any money on me when they came and arrested me. Not a cent."

"Which way do you live?"

The old man gave an address on Fair Oaks Street. It wasn't far out of his way. Neither one of them lived in the best part of town.

"I can give you a lift," Egil said.

"That's kind of you, Mr. Njalsson," Schmidts said. The mister was ironic. The arrest report hadn't given an age, just "somewhere around seventy." As far as Egil could tell that might have been off by a decade or two.

The address turned out to be a sort of second hand junk store. The operative word was junk. If the pieces in the dirty window were the best of the lot then Egil could see how Schmidts qualified as indigent.

"Thanks for the ride. I've a beer inside if you'd like."

Njalsson looked at his watch. It wasn't too early to start drinking, at least just a beer. The work at the office would wait. He had to talk to Schmidts anyway to prepare a case. Besides, the old man seemed to want to pay him back for the ride.

If anything, the shop was worse on the inside than it looked from the front. Odd bits of bric-a-brac were strewn around everywhere; most of it looking like it hadn't been moved or even dusted in twenty years. Broken down pieces of furniture were covered with moldering sheets.

The old man led him to the back and up some stairs to an apartment above the shop. The kitchen was cleaner, though still hardly spotless. Of course, Egil's own small apartment wasn't the neatest of place, either.

The refrigerator looked as old as Schmidt's, but the beer was cold. Schmidt's took out two and motioned him to a chair at the kitchen table.

"So what happens now, Mr. Njalsson?"

"The trial will be held on the date on the summons. The district attorney will call his witnesses and make his case. Then I'll make my case. The judge will then decide."

"No jury?" Schmidt's asked disappointedly.

"Not unless we've got a very strong case to present. This is a small matter. It's better left to a judge. A jury would be considered a waste of time, I'm afraid, and would probably result in a higher fine. Maybe even jail."

"So you think I'm guilty?"

"I don't think you have much of a case."

"That's different?"

"To a lawyer it is."

Schmidts snorted in disgust.

"I don't want to disillusion you, Mr. Schmidts, but you've got to face the facts. Do you have a license to practice Magic?"

"No."

"Did you tell the fortune of one Mrs. Einar Johnson?"

"Yes, and an ungrateful woman she is, too. Just because I told her the truth about that shifty salesman she thinks is going to marry her. He's just after her late husband's money."

Egil raised an eyebrow.

"It's the truth. I've been reading the cards longer than you've been alive, Mr. Njalsson, and I know what I'm doing. That salesman is the one that got her to swear out a complaint against me."

"It doesn't matter whether what you said was the truth or not. What matters is that you were practicing the Art without a license. Magic is a potentially dangerous business. It's not something that untrained people should be dealing with. That's what the law is about."

"What would you know about the Art, Mr. Lawyer?" Schmidts asked sharply.

"I know more than most, Mr. Schmidts. I studied applied metaphysics at the California Institute of Thaumaturgy for four years before going into the law. I've got a Bachelor's of Science degree. I've also got my practitioner's license from both the state of California and Wisconsin. I may not be the greatest practitioner of the Art, but I am competent enough to know what I am and am not capable of."

"So maybe you did study at a fancy school out west. Those scientists don't know everything. They think that they've discovered magic, but magic goes back. Way back. Back before Helmholtz and Gauss. Before the Egyptians and Babylonians. Magic is old, Mr. Njalsson, and the doctors and professors haven't learned half of it."

"And you have?" Egil asked sarcastically. He was getting annoyed at the old man's pretensions of knowledge. He was surprised, though, that Schmidts knew that the two physicists Helmholtz and Gauss had been instrumental in proving the scientific basis for magic.

"No. I'm no fool. I've been studying the Art all my life. I know what I know and I have a good idea of what I don't. What I do know is more than a youngster like you learns in four years at college, even if it is a fancy one."

"Look, Mr. Schmidts," Egil said. "This isn't working out. Maybe you should get yourself a different lawyer."

The old man looked at him in surprise, then shook his head. "No. I guess you were just telling me the way it is. I may not like it, but I can't fault you for telling the truth."

"Okay. Is there anything I can use in your defense?"

"Guess not."

"Well, where did you learn to tell fortunes, to read the cards?" Egil asked.

"From an old Romany woman," the old man answered.

"Where? Here in the city?"

"No, it was a long time ago. Bohemia, I think it was."

"Bohemia? You mean Czechoslovakia."

"Yes, that's what they call it now I think. Prague. I was a student there."

"A student? At a university? I thought you didn't believe in learning."

"I was younger then. I thought there were things I might learn. I was wrong."

"Did you get a degree, though? That might carry some weight, especially a foreign one."

"Wait a moment. I think I have one someplace. Let me go look." Schmidts went down to his shop. From below Egil could hear noises as if boxes were being moved around. He didn't quite know what to make of the old man's gypsy tale. Bohemia had become part of Czechoslovakia after the First World War in the breakup of the Austrian Empire. It hadn't been a separate country since the Hapsburgs.

There were footsteps on the stairway and Schmidts showed up with a small picture frame carrying a piece of parchment. It was certainly a degree, but not from the University of Prague. The writing had faded with age and Egil had never learned French, but it appeared to be a doctorate granted by the Sorbonne. It was also made out to one Jacques Krieger.

"This isn't your name."

"It was the name I was using then."

"Can you prove that?"

"Not that I can see."

"Oh well. Maybe we can use it. If you can find anymore old papers like this save them for me. We might have some defense if we can prove you had an education, particularly if it was before the current examination system went into effect."

"I'll do that, Mr. Njalsson."

"Well I've got to get going now. Can I take this with me?" the lawyer asked, holding up the sheepskin.

"Yes, if it will help."

Egil let himself out through the shop. He dumped the diploma on the car seat next to him and started the car. While the engine was warming up he glanced down at it. The date was written in Roman numerals. It took him a moment to figure out the year. It was 1847. Either the old man was lying to him or he might find himself defending him in a commitment hearing.

Also From Resurrected Press

Science Fiction Authors Resurrected

Fyfe Resurrected - The Stories of H. B. Fyfe

Stories from the Golden Age of Science Fiction by the author of *D-99*. dealing with the interaction of humans and aliens on far off worlds in ways that were as creative as they were imaginative.

Bone Resurrected - The Stories of J. F. Bone

More stories from the Golden Age of Science Fiction. Includes "The Issahar Artifact," "Assassin," "To Choke an Ocean" and more.

Nourse Resurrected - The Stories of Alan E. Nourse

Stories from the Golden Age of Science Fiction. Includes "Contamination Crew." "Coffin Cure," "The Link," and more.

Dick Resurrected - The Early Stories of Philip K. Dick

Early stories from the author of the novels that inspired "Blade Runner," "Total Recall," and through a scanner darkly. Science Fiction Authors Resurrected

OTHER CLASSIC SCIENCE FICTION NOVELS BEING RESURRECTED SOON

TALENTS, INCORPORATED - BY MURRAY LEINSTER

When a Mekinese fleet conquers his home planet, Captain Bors turns to Talents, Incorporated for help using their collection of individuals with unusual abilities to defeat the enemy and save the galaxy.

THE PIRATES OF ERSATZ - BY MURRAY LEINSTER

Bran Hodden just wanted to be an electronic engineer and marry a delightful girl. But when he's framed by the powers on Walden he's forced to turn back to his family's trade, piracy. Also published as The Pirates of Zan.

EMPIRE - BY CLIFFORD SIMAK

Spencer Chambers and Interplanetary Power owned the Solar System because they controlled the source of power. It fell to Russell Page and Harry Wilson to challenge that control if they had to cross the universe to do it.

NIGHT OF THE LONG KNIVES - THE CREATURE FROM THE CLEVELAND DEPTHS - BY FRITZ LEIBER

Two classic novellas set in the not too distant future from a classic master of science fiction.

ARMAGEDDON - 2419 A.D. - THE AIR LORDS OF HAN - BY PHILLIP FRANCIS NOWLAN

The two novels that introduced the world to that intrepid hero of the 25th Century, Buck Rogers. Buck Rogers must save the world from the clutches of the insidious Han.

Other Classic Resurrected Science Fiction
Edited by Greg Fowlkes

RESURRECTED MARTIANS
Classic Stories about Mars and Martians from the Golden Age of Science Fiction

RESURRECTED ALIENS
Classic Stories of Aliens and Alien Encounters from the Golden Age of Science Fiction

RESURRECTED FLYING SAUCERS
Classic Stories of Flying Saucers and Alien Invasions from the Golden Age of Science Fiction

RESURRECTED ROBOTS
Classic Stories of Robots, Cyborgs and Androids from the Golden Age of Science Fiction

RESURRECTED SPACE SHIPS -
Classic Stories of Space Ships from the Golden Age of Science Fiction

RESURRECTED TIME TRAVEL
Classic Stories of Time Travel from the Golden Age of Science Fiction

RESURRECTED DIMENSIONS
Classic Stories of other Dimensions from the Golden Age of Science Fiction

RESURRECTED FUTURES
Classic Stories of the Far Future from the Golden Age of Science Fiction

RESURRECTED MAD SCIENTISTS
Classic Stories of Mad Scientists and their Creations from the Golden Age of Science Fiction

RESURRECTED MONSTERS
Classic Stories of Monsters and Mayhem from the Golden Age of Science Fiction

The Fictional Detective
by Greg Fowlkes

Who killed Ezekial O. Handler?

A beautiful dame, a hard-boiled private eye – and a dead body.

It started like any other case. When a famous writer dies in a mysterious car crash, private detective Frank Slade is called in to find answers, but all he finds is more questions. Who killed Ezekial Handler? Who is Janet Nielsen and why is she so interested in finding out? Who is leaving the neatly typed clues? And as Slade tries to find answers to these questions he starts to wonder if the ultimate answer will threaten his very existence.

Read about it in
The Fictional Detective

Visit www.thefictionaldetective.com

About Resurrected Press

A division of Intrepid Ink, LLC, Resurrected Press is dedicated to bringing high quality, vintage books back into publication. See our entire catalogue and find out more at www.ResurrectedPress.com.

About Intrepid Ink, LLC

Intrepid Ink, LLC provides full publishing services to authors of fiction and non-fiction books, eBooks and websites. From editing to formatting, from publishing to marketing, Intrepid Ink gets your creative works into the hands of the people who want to read them. Find out more at www.IntrepidInk.com.

www.ingramcontent.com/pod-product-compliance
Lightning Source LLC
Chambersburg PA
CBHW061158170626
46809CB00003B/1145